BLACK BOX PROTOCOL

BETHANY LOY

FROG JONES

Impulsive
Walrus

Edited by Rhiannon Rhys-Jones

Cover Art and Design by Yoko Matsuoka

Created in cooperation with Dragondyne Publishing. The Neverwhen Roleplaying universe appears under license from Dragondyne Publishing.

To the most compassionate woman I've ever known. Grandmother, cake-maker, cattle farmer, and insatiable reader.
Norma Jean Connerly
1953-2018

Special Thanks:
Dalton Paget, a most impressive Dungeon Master, a more impressive editor. Thank you for believing in me, aiding in this work, and for being my best friend.

- Bethany Loy

ONE

THE OLD DWARF lowered my broken, scorched form down onto the red-upholstered chair. The deep, mahogany-stained wood panels of his study danced with shadows as the fireplace popped and flickered.

"Martin Aten, back in my study at last," he said, shaking his head. "Are you...I honestly don't know how to ask this... Comfortable?"

"Oh," I said. "Um...yes, I think so. At least, as comfortable as anyone can make me, right now."

Outside, the night sounded still. Comforting. In a city like Manzala, home to the magical portals that span realities, silence came at a premium. The whirring of hovercars, the beat of feet against the pavement, and the general tide of excitement and ennui that comes naturally with a large city required resources to block out. So, as I rested in the chair, I took a moment to remember that even the silence stood testimony to the vast resources at my host's disposal.

The old techno-dwarf did not sit across from me

immediately. Instead, he made his way to a small wooden bar built into one side of the room.

"Normally," he said, removing a bottle of whiskey from a rack next to the bar. "This is where I would offer an honored guest a drink. I assume, however, that your condition makes that —impractical."

Unable to even move from the chair, I chuckled wryly for a bit. "Yes," I said. "That's probably a safe assumption."

"I hope you won't mind if I—"

"No, no," I said. "Believe me—I would if I could."

The dwarf nodded, and proceeded to pour a bit of the translucent, brown liquid into a heavy-bottomed tumbler before re-corking the whiskey and placing it back on the rack. He swirled the glass a couple of times, looking mournfully at it, then closed his eyes and took a small sip. He froze, then, and even in a moment like this the corners of his mouth turned up in a slight smile before he swallowed the whiskey and nodded with approval.

"Think I needed that," he said as he walked to the chair facing mine. Between us, the fire continued its merry dance, and as he allowed himself to sink down onto the cushions, he began to regard me in earnest. His face betrayed little in the way of emotion, but after several long seconds he simply took a second drink of whiskey, then leaned back.

"So," he said. "I have some of the reports, from Altay. But...I think I'd prefer if you started at the beginning. Even the reports I have are somewhat disjointed—my operatives were in slightly better shape than you when they gave them—and even at their best I doubt they have your level of insight on the thing."

"The beginning?" I asked, pondering for a moment. "I guess the start of it was the day you contacted me, it was normal enough." I could see the vivid details of my office springing into my imagination. "I had just finished a case."

The old techno-dwarf nodded, sipped his whiskey, then leaned back in his chair as I began my tale.

TWO

My FLUSTERED CLIENT tapped his metal foot on the ragged carpet of my office. "How long's this gonna take?" the chrome-limbed man asked. He tried to frown, but only the portions of his face not covered in cybernetic enhancements managed the motion. His leather-jacketed arms made a dull clunk as he folded them over his chest, growing restless.

"You lost a Saussurea P52 motorbike, correct?" I asked, turning my screen to the customer. It displayed an entry from a local personal-sales website that my search algorithm told me was likely his bike.

His face flashed with a look of surprise as he leaned closer to the screen. "That's my ride! They painted over my decals, the bastards," he growled.

Removing my glasses to clean them, I absentmindedly began to list off the bill. "Ten for the appointment, fifteen for the time and an extra thirty if you want to know who stole it." I paused to scrutinize the glass lenses, huffed on them and continued cleaning.

"Thirty, for a name? I'll pay you for finding it, but justice should be free," my client said, grinning ear to ear, probably imagining what kind of retribution he would inflict when he found the guy.

"Revenge is priceless, but I could always get more business from his next exploit if he slips away," I observe, turning my screen back to face me.

My patron frowned stuffing his gleaming metal hands in his jacket pockets. "Fine, fifty-five for my bike and the name." he summed up.

Once he'd paid, I gave him what he wanted and the cyborg biker left to hunt down the degenerate who had stolen from him, I chuckled at the thought, imagining the biker whining about his ruined decals as he held the thief by the neck. That sort of scene was all too common in Manzala.

In a city so rife with theft, I'm never out of work as the community lost-and-found. Most of the time I'm able to find my clients' items from my office, only requiring a few simple searches with my algorithm. A look into recent pawn shop purchases, a few checks of security drones, and if the criminal is your basic, standard-issue moron, a scan of social media for bragging.

I leaned back in my chair, smiling. Easy money, if it's an algorithm and a couple key strokes. The times when I had to put foot to pavement were harder, if more interesting. I'd never figured on getting in full-on private investigator work when I started writing code, but something had to pay the bills, and the occasional security lock required my physical presence. I was just as happy that, this time, I paid the rent from the comfort of my office.

My muscles ached from the long period of

inactivity, so I rose from my chair for a moment to stretch. I stood up too quickly; my head swam for a moment, and I held on to the edge of my desk until the dizziness faded. Then I made my way to the office window.

Being on the first floor of a crowded market street meant my office didn't come with a view, but that's how I liked it. Out there, people of all kinds passed by. Some human, some dwarves, some elves. Every once in a while, an Ork or the occasional Xenoform, genetic crosses between humans and animals mixed into the crowd. Here and there, I managed to catch sight of a halfling. And, I liked to think, the odd Hylathan, dragon-descended creatures, had shapeshifted itself to blend in as one of the normal folks.

I liked observing their treks past my little venue; imagining how they lived their lives. They were nameless faces to me, but once you spend long enough in this gig you realize that under that day-to-day dreariness, every one of those faces concealed a tangled, messy web of a life. Trying to guess the nature of each at a glance had become one of my favorite pastimes.

I saw a flash on the window, and it took me a moment to realize it was a reflection from a notification light from something on my desk. "Yes, Jean?" I answered.

The light was coming from the small blackbox that I kept on my desk while I worked. The device's speaker turned on, emitting a quiet pop.

"Martin?" Jean's soft voice wavered.

I walked back to my desk and sat down. "It's me."

Jean sighed in relief, "I was worried."

"What for?" I lifted the mug on my desk to my lips, swallowing some of the bitter brew.

There was an uncomfortable silence for a moment; Jean was probably embarrassed. "For the life of me, I couldn't remember where you were." Jean said.

"I'm flattered you worry about me." I laughed. "I'm at work, but tonight I'll tell you about my day." I said.

Laughter flowed from the speaker in response, "I like your stories.".

"I know you do." I said.

...

After finding the fourth stolen Calico M950 pistol today, I was itching to head home. Entering the day's earnings into the books, I poured the last of my coffee into my mouth. I know us hard-bitten investigator types are supposed to like coffee as black and bitter as our imagined existence, but honestly the slurry of coffee and sugar that collected on the bottom of my sweetened-to-saturation cup was my favorite part. A bit of java-flavored sucrose was always good for a quick buzz. I turned off my computer, put on my jacket, and slipped the blackbox into my pocket. My keys clinked and jingled as I headed for the door.

Rain rolled off the edges of the building and slapped the concrete sidewalk as I locked the door to my office. Pulling my hood up over my short, gray hair, I turned towards the busy street, only to be blocked by a black-suited droid. I was a bit taken aback at first, to see what looked like a cheap, service-level machine dressed in professional attire, but when it didn't respond to my wave, I brought my attention back to the route home. Two steps around the stylish robot was all I managed before it spoke.

"Mr. Aten, may I have a word with you?" it said, not even turning its optic receptors to face me.

What a great way to set someone on edge. Whoever owned this automaton clearly didn't invest any time into making its behavior less unsettling. Letting the hairs on the back of my neck settle, I said "Sorry, just closed up shop, bud."

The thing's head whirred as it processed the information. "It is quite urgent, Dr. Glenmont has requested your services." it said.

Raising my bushy eyebrows in surprise I responded. "Dr. Glenmont? As in, *the* Dr. Glenmont? Edis Incorporated?"

Whirring again, "Yes," the droid answered. It turned and motioned to a car.

Along the sidewalks of the dampened street, pedestrians hurried to-and-fro. A fashionable, brightly-garbed dwarf strutting on tall platform shoes gave a curious glance towards the droid as he passed a gray ork who had an expression of boredom on his face while wearing a delivery uniform and going the other direction. If anyone paid the machine any attention, it was a passing interest.

Service bots were commonplace on construction sites or in overalls doing janitorial work; one in a suit would draw anyone's eye. Manzala's place as a nexus between worlds makes it a hub for the bizarre, though, so most of us locals learn to swallow our curiosity and move along. If you see a service droid in a suit on the street, you continue on your way. If said droid brings up Dr. Glenmont, it's time to stop and ask questions.

Digging my hands into my jacket pockets, I retrieved my experi-sense kit. Opening the little pouch, I clipped the tiny camera onto the frame of my glasses, and pressed the black, quarter-sized Emoti-Sense add-on to my right upper cheek bone, where it adhered to my skin right above my trim grey goatee. Then I connected both Sense Feeds to the blackbox.

I clicked 'Record' on the side of the blackbox with my index finger. "If anything, this will make for an interesting story." I said.

...

Manzala has its celebrities, but Dr. Glenmont is a different story entirely. There are those who can't shut up about him, his inventions, and the way he provided much of the city's wonders. Others hate his guts, claiming him a fraud who steals credit and ideas, a brutal capitalist who isn't above sabotaging other inventors, so on and so forth. Whatever you believe, his influence on the city cannot be denied. Buildings, vehicles, weapons, you name it, he had a hand in making it possible.

The car the robot invited me into parked in front of Glenmont's towering estate in the New Town district, and another suited service bot waiting in front of the gate stepped up and opened the car door for me.

Politely bowing, the robot graciously said "Welcome sir. Please follow me to Dr. Glenmont."

Beyond the ornate metal gate I could see the front yard, a pleasant grove of trees, bushes and flowers. The plant life blocked the view of the main building except the one feature all of Manzala was familiar with, the massive tower reaching up into the clouds. I've never understood the propensity of techno-dwarves to prefer spending their days in gleaming ivory towers of their own making. The metal monolith just looks like a prison to me.

My excitement fluttered in my stomach as the gate opened. During the ride, I had asked the original service bot in the driver's seat "What business does Glenmont have for me?"

No matter how I phrased my questions, it only responded with things like "I was only to deliver you to Dr. Glenmont. My apologies that I cannot answer such questions."

My mind raced at the thought of the possibilities. Had the famous inventor-magnate taken an interest in my programming? Being led through the trees, I tried to take in as much of the carefully manicured environment as I could. A small green bird flew overhead, but I quickly pegged it as a camouflaged security drone. Unfortunately for my business, but fortunately for my sense of privacy, such drones are only legal on private property. The citizens would be up in arms if any random bird on a power line could be a hidden surveillance device, spying on their every move. But they don't seem to mind the security cameras that are almost as ubiquitous. People like their government observers to be obvious, I guess. Apparently, that makes it OK.

The machine servant opened the front door and motioned me in. Stepping through the doorway, I paused a moment as my eyes adjusted to the indoor lighting. Hardwood flooring, high ceilings, aesthetically pleasing furniture, It surprised me that the decorum of the main lobby was no different from my expectations of a rich man's home. Like the pictures in a home designer's magazine, the room showed no individuality; it didn't even look lived in.

As I was led down a hallway, I felt the blackbox in my pocket vibrating rhythmically. Jean was trying to get a hold of me again.

This wasn't the best time to talk, but I could at least open up my experi-sense camera feed for her to watch. Slipping my hand into my pocket, I flipped the small switch on the blackbox to open the feed. One door ahead was ajar, light shining through the gap.

The droid led me to the door ajar and pushed it the rest of the way open. I followed into a study, which unlike the front lobby, was a complete mess. Not the disorganization of use over a long period of time, but the whirlwind of a recent tantrum. Books were strewn across the floor, a lamp had been knocked off an end table. At the other end of the room, in a sturdy wooden chair, sat a frazzled dwarf with his head in his hands. My previous excitement was replaced with a pit in my stomach.

Without looking up, Glenmont spoke "As I

11

understand it, you have a policy of confidentiality?" the man sat there, still as a statue.

"...Absolutely." Quickly and quietly, I detached the camera and Emoti-sense pad, slipping them into the pouch in my pocket. "I'd only set up my experi-sense as a security measure, but-".

Glenmont's head shot up and stared straight into my eyes. Interrupting me with his piercing green gaze, scanning my features for any sign of deception. "Do I have your promise that not one word or piece of data will reach the public?"

That wasn't the sort of question that usually preceded a simple job. I tried to give the most reassuring look at my disposal, thinking *"The hell did I walk into?"*

"You have my word, sir." I said.

The dwarf's searching look eased and he motioned to the chair in front of his. I sat down, folding my hands together on my lap. *Calm down*, I thought to myself.

"You have a reputation, Mr. Aten. They say that you can find anything you put your mind towards. You also are known not—and I'm trying to think of the best way to phrase this—to be a bastard. You're the type to have enough foresight not to stab someone like me in the back." Glenmont said, leaning forward. His face had assumed a threatening glare, but his voice had more than a hint of desperation to it, and that combined with abnormality of my summons led me to conclude that Dr. Glenmont was panicked about —something.

"A lot of money could be made, leaking information to my rivals. However..." his piercing eyes flickered to my face again. For a dwarf with a shaved face, he was surprisingly intimidating.

After a moment of silence, during which I couldn't find the courage to do more than nod, he continued. "I need you to find my Dwarven Engine."

A shock ran through my body as I comprehended his words, and any fatigue my mind had been experiencing was replaced with instant alarm. It was no wonder Glenmont was in such an emotional state; he'd lost his life's work. Of all precious things he could lose, his inventions, his treasures, his fortune, this was the one thing that any techno-dwarf would cut off a leg to save.

Any of us who work with tech know a thing or two about techno-dwarves. We know, for instance, that a Dwarven Engine is an important part of every techno-dwarf's life. It's an obsession, and a rite of passage. Like Glenmont, all techno-dwarves are inventors to some degree. Much of the technology the average citizen of Manzala relies on stems from their secrets—including the surveillance gear I'd just detached. But their engines—those are a technology closely guarded, understood only by them, and to the rest of us they may as well work by magic. A Techno-Dwarf's engine could enhance any machine, making it run bigger, better, faster, and none of us who weren't born to that life had any idea how.

Many would benefit from the use of a Dwarven Engine, but since their inventors refuse to share their secrets, getting any use from a purchased or stolen engine would be nigh impossible without a techno-dwarf to operate it. But that didn't keep rich idiots from occasionally buying them to try to reverse-engineer one, or criminals from holding their inventor's most prized possessions for ransom. That latter struck me as a real possibility, given Dr. Glenmont's prominent wealth.

"Has anyone tried to contact you about the engine?" I asked.

Glenmont clenched his fists, "Not a peep." he said. He began to grind his teeth in frustration, and his glare directed itself away from me, and toward some nameless thief. The anger in the room was just this side of palpable.

That ruled out ransom, then. But if you were going to try to steal an Engine for profit...why this one? Why the techno-dwarf with more resources than any other to bring down upon your head? The risks staggered me.

The doctor was right to be concerned about my discretion; if word of this got out, his indomitable reputation would be badly shaken. The entire city might feel the effects of that. *Jean will be disappointed that I have to cancel date night tonight.* I thought to myself.

"How did this happen?" I said. "I have to assume you have precautions against this kind of thing."

Glenmont looked off, his gaze a lightyear away, then stood up and walked towards the door. "Follow me, Mr. Aten." opening the door and turning to the droid outside the door "Grab me a whiskey, will you? Single-malt, slightly peated?"

The droid bowed and walked away. Glenmont

brought up his hands to smooth down the wild strands of brown and grey hair. He had aged very graciously; those who didn't know him well would be surprised to find out that he was well into his second century. I was a tad envious, given that I, at sixty-seven, had lost my hue long ago.

I realized that he was waiting for me, so I quickly got up and followed after Glenmont down the narrow halls of his home.

...

The polished stone blocks, laid in countless, precisely measured rows that formed the daunting architecture of Glenmont's tower now rested beneath my feet. The excitement I felt standing atop such a monument was paralleled by the growing sense of unease I had felt building with every floor in the elevator ride up to this room. The feeling of being trapped in the empty sky. If not for the fresh air flowing in from the large shattered window, I would have found it difficult to breath. I shivered as I considered the drop, and could feel goosebumps rising on my skin.

Even though the room had been airing out since the break in, a perturbing smell lingered in the air. With every step further in, more of it wafted into my nose. I strained my olfactory senses, but I didn't recognize it, though I noticed an oily texture clinging to my nostrils.

Observing the circular room that was Glenmont's tower laboratory, I waited for my folding portable computer to finish the usual algorithm searches through Manzala's various networks. I didn't expect to find all that much, not for a job like this, but it didn't hurt to try and maintaining a sense of professionalism helps when dealing with chaos. Work tables and shelving lined the stone walls. To the right of the window the inventor's manuals were shelved. Some papers littered the ground, a sign that the shelves had been rifled through.

"Are any of these missing?" I said, pointing at the small library.

"No," Glenmont said, taking a swig of the whiskey in his hand. "Perused, but not taken. Mongrel must have thought I would be idiotic enough to make a manual for my engine."

A tone from my portable computer, which I'd set up on one of the rare empty spaces on one of the many desks, told me that it had completed its search.

"So...we can rule out another techno-dwarf doing this?" I asked, picking the device up to look over the results.

"Not that I'd believe one of our people could do such a thing." he said assuredly, shaking his head. "I would never do this to one of my own kind, even with a gun to my head"

I looked through the search algorithm's results. None of the neighboring properties' security cameras or drones caught anything unusual in the time window. That surprised me—usually there would be *something* to go on, if not much. Then I reviewed their search patterns and camera arcs, and quickly realized that they'd all carefully excluded any direct view of the techno-dwarf's tower. I imagine Glenmont must have paid handsomely to establish such a blind spot. The famous inventor must have been paranoid about his rivals using these surveillance feeds to spy on him, but by protecting himself from that, he may have opened himself up to other malicious acts.

"Did your security catch anything?" I asked.

Letting out an exasperated sigh, he looked up at me. "The proximity sensors went off, along with the alarm in the window, but the camera drones recorded nothing, though several of them were blinded with a laser glare just before the window shattered. It was a smash and grab, over in seconds." He pressed his fingers against his brow in frustration. "The sentry gun fired three shots before it was taken out, none of them hit. Worthless."

"Experienced," I said, "and well-equipped. He'd studied you, and his target." I looked up to see a torn-open ball turret protruding from the ceiling, its laser barrel still dangling from a loose wire. "Now, question is—solo job, or work for hire" I said, more to myself than anything. I followed this with a long "Hmmmm," letting my most recent and most wealthy employer hear how stumped I was. So much for professionalism.

I double-checked through the algorithm results. Nothing from pawn shops, but that was to be expected. Dwarven Engines were unique devices, most of the owners of which would drop everything in an effort to recover them. That meant that if someone was trying to sell one, it was either taken off of a techno-dwarf's corpse or was being pursued by an short ball of flesh, machinery, and rage that nobody wants to get on the wrong side of. That made it too hot an item even for most black markets.

Either we were looking for an extremely skilled idiot who was under the impression that he could sell it at a high price at the local fence, or he already had a buyer lined up.

"Where did you keep the engine?" I asked.

Glenmont strode to the far left wall, opening a small cabinet above the desk to reveal a large, gleaming, steel safe, the remains of a biometric locking system still cling to the front. The safe's door had been slashed open in a long streak, cutting through the inch-thick plating, the locking bars, and leaving a deep gouge on the inside of the inner plate. To do that so quickly and efficiently... I raised my eyebrows in disbelief. Walking over to the cabinet, I peered closely at the gouge.

"No noticeable residues of acid or other corrosive chemicals. It's clearly a cut, far too clean for an explosive blast. No shavings left over, so a repetitive motion like from a rotary tool is out of the question." I said, bewildered. "I think this was done in one, terrifying swing of some kind of blade."

The smell, ever present through the room, was strongest in front of the safe. I was starting worry this unpleasant stench would latch onto my clothing. I shook my head; I needed to focus. "So, we have someone who somehow got up to the tower window fast enough not to be seen, broke in, destroyed your sentry turret, rifled through your collection of technical manuals, and cut through your safe like butter. Then they made off with your engine, either by descending back through the window and crossing the grounds within seconds, flying off behind the trees, or disappearing into thin air."

This criminal seemed unlikely to start posting online about his deeds for street cred. I didn't know what to make of any of the limited clues the perpetrator had left behind. I examined the inside of the empty safe, then began to close the safe door, but something rattled in the hollow space between the plates. Borrowing a pair of long tweezers from the Doctor's workbench and producing a finger-sized flashlight from my pocket, I reached into the jagged hole. A shiny little shard of something glinted in the light at the bottom of the little hollow, and I plucked it out carefully and held it up for Dr. Glenmont to see.

Glenmont put his glass down on a bench as he walked over, glaring at the blue scale. He leaned in, pulling a magnifying lens from one of his pockets. "Slithering, shapeshifting cretin," he growled.

I grinned, chuckling darkly. "Now to find the hylathan in the haystack."

...

Glenmont lent me one of his cars to keep me from wasting any more time going back home to get my own. Finding a reptile who can disguise himself as any other species in a city with what were presumably quite a few of the same—getting a count had always been difficult given the average hylathan's desire to pass as anything but what they were—was going to be difficult. But there were ways, and the first of them was old friend of mine, a man named Sylvester.

My coat pocket vibrated. Jean was trying to call.

Keeping my eyes on the road I quickly took out the blackbox and answered it.

"Hello, there." I said, turning left onto the Old Town Ziggurat Freeway.

Manzala proper had been built upon gargantuan ancient stepped pyramids. This made traveling from district to district annoyingly complicated. I looked up to see the countless hovercars floating above the ground traffic without a care to their destinations--they had it easy, but those of us who counted our credits needed to take a more circuitous route.

"Where are you, dear?" Jean asked, her voice strained with anxiety. "What... was going on just now?"

I felt a pang of guilt. I'd opened the Sense-Feed to her, only to suddenly shut it off when I caught sight of the state of my client.

"Everything's okay, love. But...I'm working on a case for Dr. Glenmont, so date night isn't going to work out. Sorry about that." I said.

"Glenmont?" Jean said excitedly. "I know that name!"

"Yes, the Greatest Inventor himself has me on a case." I said, I noticed a cab in my rearview mirror, tailgating me.

"Glenmont, he was the dwarf you saw? The one who looked so upset?" Jean asked.

"Something very dear to him was stolen." I told her, eyeing the cab, which was still tailing to close for comfort. The windows were tinted, but I could see the snout of a hound poking out from the passenger side window. Odd for a cabbie to drive with a pet.

"That's too bad. Don't worry about me, I can wait to hear this story until after you know how it ends." Jean said.

I imagined Jean's brilliant smile on the other end of the line. She was always so quick to forgive me and my inconveniences; she had always been too good for me.

The cabbie moved to the fast lane and began to pass me. I looked to see if I could recognize the breed of dog, but the window was rolled up now.

"I'll regale you with the tale soon enough." I said.

Laughter flowed from the speaker in response, "I love your stories.".

"I know you do." I said, hanging up to focus on the road.

...

The strobing lights and flickering mirror ball of Cosmos-a-Go-Go gave me a blaring headache the moment I walked in the door. The patrons of the bar—most of which were maybe half my age, if that —gyrated to the sounds to canned music and Sylvester's voice. He stood on the small bar stage, that slightly-curly hair of his bouncing over the chestnut skin of his forehead as he gyrated to his own singing. The shimmering glitter of his pink outfit reflected the pulsing lights, and the crowd cheered him on as he belted out an overdone disco tune. I shook my head and headed for one of the corner booths—darker, and with a bit of acoustic shielding. They were the clubs one concession to the notion that not all of their customers were hormone-driven tweenies looking for booze and a one-night stand.

As Sylvester finished his song and the music trailed off, he looked out at the audience with a bright smile. Everyone was a friend of Sylvester's, yet somehow he managed to make you feel special just for knowing him.

He was one in a million, and his love of life and sensation made him an excellent source on all kinds of drugs. If you wanted a narcotic, psychedelic, or stimulant, you name it and he knew who to talk to. Hylathan pheromones were obscure, but if anyone in Manzala knew where someone might source a supply, it would be Sylvester.

Sylvester sat down across from me, he leaned in and dramatically sniffed the air. "*Love* your new cologne," he said in his soprano voice, leaning back with a huge smile. "Who's the lucky lizard girl?"

"Lizard man." I corrected, smirking. I was right to come here first.

Sylvester's eyebrows shot up in surprise, his lips parted into a toothy grin. "Mm, mm, mm—after all my efforts. Who would've thought-"

I put my hand up, "It's for a case. I accidentally picked this 'Cologne' up trying to locate a perp." I said.

Sylvester's face dropped into a pout, "And here I thought, just for once, you might be here for pleasure instead of business. Martin, I keep telling you that you gotta get out there, live your life, and you got my hopes up, man! Now here I am thinking that you've gone and found love in a pair of scaly arms and leathery wings, and nah, you're just chasing after another perp." He threw his hands up in frustration.

"You know that my Jean wouldn't approve of your kind of 'fun'."

"Jean," he huffed sarcastically, rolling his eyes. Then he shook his head, forcing a smile back. "Alright, I understand."

I let out a sigh, and looked back up. "Look, I need your help with this one, Syl. It's a unique case." I said.

He waved his hand in a disappointed gesture; I chose to interpret it as consent.

"It's my usual speciality," I said. "A stolen item. Burglary, this time, but the burglar had to have been using a heavy dose of pheromones. He cut through a safe with just his claws."

Sylverster leaned forward intently on this. "What kinda safe are we talking, like a hotel safe, or...?"

I shook my head. "Inch thick steel plates, Good steel, too." I responded.

"He would have needed a super-concentrated dose for that. I mean, I've been with a Hylathan who took a dose of pheromones first, and it made him a beast, but it wasn't quite to the point where I was worried about him ripping my arms off in the moment," said Sylvester.

I gave my head a wry shake. "I know Hylathans can use it as a performance enhancer, and the room he broke into reeked of the stuff. What you smell on me is what I got from just walking through the place."

He raised his eyebrows at that. "He must have

been a beast already to start with, but that's a lot more than your typical street dose."

He chewed on his lip as he thought about it. "It's difficult to get your hands on more than a little bit at a time. Lots of the lizards sell their sweat on the side, but for that much, you're looking for a specialized dealer." Then he lit up with a smile. "So, you're in luck. I know a guy who deals in bulk." Sylvester leaned forward, propping his chin on one hand and winked. "I'll send you his address," he said, then got a funny little smile. "Now, for my payment..."

I began to pull out my Credit Stick, but he shook his head at me as I did. "Your money's no good here. I've got somethin' else in mind." He gestured to the stage behind him. "Play a song with me. Up on stage. You can just play your guitar. We'll make a show of it, it'll be great!"

"I will, after the-" I was interrupted by my blackbox vibrating.

I pulled the device out to answer it when Sylvester reached across the table, pressing his hand over mine while I held it. He looked from the box to me with a pained expression.

"Hey..." he said softly, slowly removing his hand from mine. His brow creased as he said, "Look man, I've done a little bit of everything, but I'll never do heroin again."

A shock ran down my spine, "What, I-" He raised his hand open palmed to signal me to stop.

He clasped his hands together on the table. "Heroin," he said, eying the blackbox pointedly. "It's not for parties, it's for avoiding things. Mostly, it's for avoiding the exact parts of life that a person needs to go through the most if they're going to get to the rest of it."

Anger welled up in my gut, along with heat to my face. I was shaking a little, but my voice was cold. "This *is* the rest of my life." I snatched the Box to my chest and stood up, staring him down. "I'm not like you, Syl."

Sylvester didn't move at all. He coldly eyed me for a moment, then wordlessly scratched a name and an address down on a piece of paper and handed it to me.

Stomping towards Glenmont's car, I tried to push Sylvester's words from my mind. Focus on the case, that's what's important. Now that I had the dealer, it was simple as asking him who'd bought a huge batch of pheromones. I might have to loosen his lips with some credits, but that was nothing new. In Manzala everything has a price.

As I reached out my hand to the car door, a clawed hand reached from behind me to hold it closed. My heart leapt into my throat. I was so distracted I hadn't been on guard at all. Dread knotted up in my stomach, the memory of the claw marks in the safe raced through my mind as I looked up.

I saw a dark silhouette with a long muzzle against the sun, and then his other hand swung around and clocked me on the side of the head. My world went blurry and I felt my knees buckle under me, everything going sideways before it all went dark.

THREE

My breath came out in soft, white clouds as I walked along the frozen path. All my muscles tensed--out of anxiety, not because of the bone-chilling weather. It had been months since last I'd visited. Nearly two feet of packed snow spread out across the cemetery and my worry grew as I realized that the groundskeeper hadn't cleared the site.

If one didn't know any better, the field could be easily confused for a small park. Hanging icicles decorated its trees and bushes, and only a few heavily plumed geese still resided here. A large snow berm was left where the groundskeeper had decided he had cleared enough pathway. The flat grave markers hadn't left recognizable divots to identify where they lay. My stomach dropped, *'Did I come here for nothing?'* I thought.

Clenching my fists, I reassured myself thinking *'No, I remember where it is.'*

I trudged on, each step sinking deep, the snow crunching under my feet. The first few inches of snow had frozen through and more resembled jagged ice.

"I'm sure it's this way. I have to remember where the grave is." I thought, as I wandered through the frozen wasteland.

However, with each step my unease transformed into self-loathing. "Come on, I've been here a hundred times. I can't have forgotten where it is." I told myself.

Looking around frantically trying to identify anything in the white expanse to no avail, I stomped three steps forward.

"Here!" I blurted out. *"It has to be here!"* I stooped down and began to dig with my hands.

The layers of ice were too hard to scrape away with my fingers. "Dammit. Dammit. Dammit!" I screamed, as I punched down trying to break though. Pain shot through my arm, the jagged ice scratched my hands and my knuckles ached from the cold collision with the ground.

The realization hit me like a falling anvil. *"I can't find it!"* The weight of the thought seemed to push down on my shoulder blades; I could barely hold myself up. My knees sunk into the snow. I was blinded by the building tears. My breath hiccupped in and out as I held back sobs.

'Clearly, you didn't love her enough to remember.' the darkest part of me sneered.

...

The sound of screeching mechanical brakes penetrated my ears, jolting me from my nightmare, and my body jostled forward. My arms slid against

27

the leather material in front of me. Before the visions of frozen graves could abandon me completely, I fell forward, smacking my head on the carpeted floor. The impact to my skull left me with a sense of deja-vu, and I tensed with panic.

I appeared to have fallen off into the space between the front and back seats of a car. Glenmont's? I couldn't be sure. A cold sweat formed on my brow. I could feel the car's jerky acceleration, and every sharp turn caused me to sway in one direction or another. *My god*, I thought. If my kidnapper intended to keep me alive; what else did he have in store for me? What did he want, and what would he be willing to do to me to get it? My mind rushed through every conceivable nightmare my captor could be planning, but the list was both endless and futile.

Trying to stay as still as possible, I considered my options. Jump out of a moving vehicle? Tell him everything I knew and beg for my life? Try attacking him from the back seat? What if he had a gun, a partner in crime in the car? The combination of intense driving, stress, and whatever someone had done to my head earlier left me with a blinding headache and terrible motion sickness.

The nausea came in wave after wave; each wave felt like it rocked my guts back and forth, leaving me with a growing dizziness, and a suspicion that I had a concussion. Moving as cautiously as I could, I turned my head to take a peek between the seats at the driver.

I first saw his hands; huge, black, fur-covered things wrapped around the steering wheel, with shaggy fur hanging down from his wrists. My gaze following the length of his thick arms, covered in white fur with the occasional black splotch, to his barrel chest hidden behind a green T-shirt. He was a canine xenoform, and his shaggy fur only added to his intimidating bulk, though his long drooping ears and jowls seemed more disarming as I caught sight of his face through the mirror. He looked almost exactly like a Newfoundland.

Strong, perceptive, and determined, the larger dog xenoforms are difficult to contend with. I briefly re-considered my option of jumping out of the moving vehicle as an alternative to confronting him.

Before I could even plan my next move, the car swerved, and motion sickness overcame me. The coffee I had enjoyed earlier today rocketed up my esophagus, my cheeks puffed as I tried to contain it all in my mouth, but to no avail. I gagged one final time, then the acidic collection of coffee and bile launched all over the backseat's carpet.

"Shit," my canine captor said, shifting his weight towards the window and sticking his muzzle out into the clean air. The smell was bad enough for me; it gave me some small sense of schadenfreude to know that he had the far more sensitive nose.

He rolled down the window and cocked his muzzle towards the fresh air. I remembered the cab behind me on my way to Sylvester; it was the same damn dog. How long had he been following me?

With another swerve behind a high wall, and a sudden stop, I retched again, though my stomach contained nothing else with which to coat his upholstery. The Dog jumped out of the car, throwing the back door open and grasping for my leg.

Uselessly kicking my legs, I tried to speak between dry heaves. "It—it's just a job! I'll stop searching, I'll-" my gag reflex interrupted my speech; being on my side didn't make it easy to keep anything down.

With a firm grasp on my ankle he tugged, pulling me relentlessly out. Frantically grasping for a handhold, I continued to cough and sputter. With my other leg I kicked and kicked, one blind strike making contact with my assailant's shoulder.

He growled angrily, pulling even harder now, but shifting to put his body out of range of my flailing leg. "You. Will. Tell. Me!" he said, enunciating each word with a hard yank on my ankle.

I tried grabbing the back of the driver's seat, but my hands slipped across the sleek upholstery and I was pulled further out of the car. He got hold of my other leg at the knee, and lifted me like a human wheelbarrow as my hands scrambled over the leather seat. As I left the car, I made a desperate grab for the door and latched on to the inner handle, clinging to it as the son of a bitch held me several feet off the ground.

"Help. Help!" I choked out, gasping, my knuckles turning ghost white in my desperate grip.

"Raaaah" the Dog growled, yanking again and again. "Rip yer' goddamned legs off!"

Searing pain throughout my shoulders told me if this continued, one of them would dislocate. "Stop! Please, stop!" I screamed.

"Where is he!" he said.

"Who?" I asked.

Losing the last of my grip, his final tug sent the both of us flying back. I heard him slam his back into the wall behind him, the air in his lungs pressed out in a yelp. My side slapped the concrete painfully, as the rest of me flopped down as well. He wheezed as I pushed myself onto my feet. Walls rose high on either side of the car, and it became clear he'd pulled into a cramped, deserted alley way.

I started limping my way towards the road.

A hand clutched the back of my jacket and pulled me back before I could leave the alley. Twisting me around to face him with a hand on my shoulder, the Dog slammed me against the wall and furiously snarled in my face "My brother! Where is he?"

"Brother? Wha-" before I could finish, he started shaking me violently.

"No lies! I know you know! Last time I saw 'em he had yer' scent on 'em!" he said.

I stuttered incomprehensibly, having trouble making sense of what he was saying. Shaking me again he raised one hand in a fist, "Speak!" he roared, his muzzle flashing open to show off his glistening, pointed teeth.

"Y-y-your brothers a lizard?" I said.

He blinked with confusion, "What? No!" he took a moment to compose himself. "Brother's a human. Lots'o tech implants. Came to see you fer one of his med-trials." His anger rose up, and he slammed me against the wall again, glaring directly into my eyes. "Didn't come home. Said the job was 'sketchy', and didn't come home!" He smashed his fist into my side, my left kidney felt the brunt of it. "Where did you take 'em?"

In reaction to the pain, I curled forward. "I don't know..."

He jabbed me again, then brought his fist back, ready for another strike. "Stop. Lying!"

I held up a placating hand. "W-wait! This scent, it isn't mine, it's from a—A Hylathan!" I gasped for breath.

He blinked, cocking his head to the side, his grip on my shirt going lax. "Fer real?" he asked as he tilted his head. His eyes shifting from anger to worried doubt. "Never did smell a human like that."

"This scent, It's from the scene of a crime. A theft. I'm investigating, trying to find the thief." I said, grateful that at least the beating had stopped.

The canine's intense stare convinced me to keep talking.

My head throbbed, "The guy I'm looking for, the thief, they must have met your brother after, if you're right about this scent being on him." I said.

He searched my eyes with his for a moment, then relaxed his grip on me, nodding his head. He tapped the end of his muzzle. "Nose ain't wrong," he said.

...

Back in Glenmont's car with my former kidnapper, with me in the passenger seat and him driving, we were headed towards the pheromone dealer. I had explained the situation to him as best I could, it didn't dispel all distrust, but at least now he was inclined to work with me.

As he drove, the silence between us became more and more awkward. To clear the air I said "Name's Martin." with a shrug of my shoulders.

His ears perked up a little, "Bosun" he replied. He gave me quick glance, then looked back at the road.

A full-on migraine was forming behind my eyes, so I lowered the sun visor and checked myself in its mirror. A purple-and-yellow bruise hiblited the swelling on my left eye and my bottom lip was split. I pressed my bent, scratched glasses up my face, the frame painfully grazing the bruises on the bridge of my nose.

Bosun's ears flattened back at the sound, "Sorry fer' the lumps I gave ya" he said in his deep, rough voice. His hands tensed for a moment, a guilty look crossed his visage.

His apology took me by surprise. After a moment of consideration, I said "It'll heal" and turned to give him a reassuring smile.

He quickly glanced at me, the corner of his mouth turned upward in response. Then he turned his head back to facing the road. I couldn't help but to relax a little, knowing I had eased things between Bosun and I, at least to a small degree. I leaned back in my seat and watched the pavement outside roll past, letting go of at least some of my body's tension.

That's when the screen in the middle of the dashboard lit up and Glenmont's face appeared. Heat rushed to my cheeks as I realized he was video calling, and he could see us just as well as we could see him. I sat straight up, the muscle tension flaring up again.

Glenmont squinted at Bosun, face turning beet

red. "Who the hell-" he turned his focus to my face and the color drained from his. After a few moments he whispered "How much?".

Bosun's eyebrows and ears raised up high in surprise, "What?" he replied.

Glenmont stared daggers at Bosun, and said in a flat, rigid tone, "How much to guarantee his safety?"

Bosun's eyes crinkled at the corners, as he laughed heartily. He turned his head to face me "Yer story checks out. The Dr. Glenmont!"

Bosun wasn't paying attention to the road as he laughed. I found this particularly concerning, given that we were approaching the vehicle ahead of us at a frighteningly high speed. I stiffened in anticipation of a wreck.

The big canine xenoform noticed our danger at the last moment and swerved into the next lane. The G-force violently pulled me to the left as we missed the car ahead of us by inches. He was grinning ear to ear, looking back and forth from me to the road. His tail was wriggling in what little space it had between the seat and his back.

Glenmont was wide eyed with shock, "Maniac mutt, you listen here!"

"Sorry about yer engine, sir" Bosun said, as he cut off an Implant-Mechanic's commercial van.

The van's horn blared in annoyance as it swerved, seeming to break Bosun's cheerful demeanor. His expression turned into a serious scowl, "I lost somethin' too. Me and Martin are workin' together."

Glenmont looked dumbfounded with his mouth slightly agape, he looked to me expectantly.

I raked my short hair back and grimaced sheepishly, "His brother had the same scent left at your tower, before going missing. Bosun confused me for a bad guy and we had a... small disagreement. It's likely that both of your cases are connected." I said.

Bosun nodded his head in agreement, and his tongue lolled out a bit to the side of his mouth.

With eyebrows raised Glenmont stared at the two of us. After a moment he rubbed his face with his hand, like an attempt to wipe away the stress. "He'll keep his mouth shut?" he asked.

"On my word, sir." Bosun said.

Glenmont sighed with frustration, letting his shoulders slump down. "And how much is you word worth?" he said.

"As much as my brother's safety," Bosun clenched his hands, firmly gripping the steering wheel. His brow creased with intense worry, "However much yer' engine's worth to you, finding him is life and death fer' me."

The renowned inventor closed his eyes, and sighed again. He looked resigned to his fate, "Send me your identification information, if you give me any reason to believe-"

"On my word." Bosun repeated, interrupting Glenmont.

The distressed Glenmont stared hard at Bosun, it looked like he was deciding whether to believe him or not. He nodded, then directed his gaze to me, "And what progress have you seen so far," he gave a sidelong glance at Bosun, "Other than your new... comrade?"

"We're headed for the only pheromone dealer

capable of supplying the thief with a dose strong enough to get him into your tower." I said.

Glenmont straightened, gaining back some of his confidence from my answer. "Very good. Keep me updated." With that, he closed the call.

Bosun blinked, nonplussed for a second, then smiled with the release of anxiety. He glanced at me, his tail wagging again; he had the jitters from sheer anticipation.

I took out my netbook, "First off, send your info to Glenmont, so we can ease his mind. Then tell me about this brother of yours. I'll do some database searches on the way." I said.

Bosun's teeth glinted as he smiled radiantly, "Will do. Big brother's name is Gordon, he's gonna be struck dumb find'in out I spoke to Glenmont."

...

'Gordon Baron, Human Male, twenty six in age, has a criminal record, but nothing major.' I continued reading the search results on my computer, as Bosun drove. 'A theft charge here, vandalism there, common symptoms of those born in the impoverished portions of the city. Being below the poverty line helped explain why Gordon was partaking in 'sketchy' jobs'.

Bosun made the final turn and parked in front of 'Golden Flamingo Pawn.' The building's front was framed by a row of bicycles so rusted I couldn't imagine anyone buying them for anything but scrap metal. The fence, the doors, even the sign out front screamed 'impending tetanus shot,' and I could not for the life of me figure out whether the sign out front reading "Laser Blades Half Off, Free Grenade With Every Missing Finger" was a novelty item or an actual offer from the shop. There was no way for this business to be successful as a pawn shop— which made it just about perfect as a front for a drug dealer.

"Yer computer find anythin'?" Bosun asked, as his nose twitched trying to catch a sent.

I put my computer away as I answered, "Unfortunately, no."

His ears drooped further down in disappointment, he opened the car door and stepped out. His body immediately went stiff as a rail, his ears rising high up along with his tail and the ruff of fur on the back of his neck. "I smell it." He said.

There's a moment, before a wild animal dashes off in pursuit. Bosun's muscles tensed, and his gaze fixed on the pawn-shop door. I flowed from the car and put a hand on his shoulder, interrupting this disastrous train of impending action. "Here's an idea," I said in an overly-gentle voice, as though trying to calm a wild animal and not a sentient being. "I'll do the talking and you'll be the muscle if muscle becomes necessary."

Bosun exhaled in something between a snort and a sigh, but the ruff of fur lowered somewhat as he turned to me. "If ya' say so." He said, crossing his arms over his green t-shirt.

The grungy, florescent-lit shop was lined from floor to ceiling with shelves of mismatched items. A film of dust coated almost every shelf in the place, and a series of greasy-looking stains decorated the linoleum floor. I didn't know how they'd managed to make the inside of this shop *less* appealing than the outside, but there it was.

Bosun's hair began to rise back up on end, his nose twitching wildly. I strode ahead. A middle-aged looking man sat at the front counter, his receding hairline made more prominent by the thorough greasing-back of each strand of hair. He eyed the two of us, as we came up.

Bosun stared intently at the man. I bumped his side with my elbow in hopes of snapping him out of it. He jumped a little, realization dawning on his face, he sheepishly strode to the pocket knives display on the left wall.

I faced the pawnbroker, "Hello, I'm-"

The potbellied shop-keep interrupted me, "I know, you're that Lost And Found guy. Listen, the shit I'm sellin' ain't stolen." He looked at his nails and absentmindedly picked at them. Finding a hangnail, he brought his hand to his mouth to bite at it.

My skin crawled with disgust. "I'm actually here for information on Hylathan pheromones, I was told you sell them." I said.

His eyes flicked to mine, "What kind of info?" he said.

"The names of your most recent buyers" I said.

"Not fuckin' happening, pal" The repulsive shopkeep replied, furrowing his brow.

"Three hundred credits." I offered.

"Chump change. Do you know what my customers would do if they heard I had loose lips? I'd be lucky if a Molotov didn't crash through my window." He sneered.

My headache started to return in full force, a

reminder of my earlier injuries. I looked at Bosun, an idea taking shape in my mind. I pointed at the giant Xenoform, "Do you know him?" I asked.

The man leaned over the counter to look at Bosun, "No, should I?" he leaned back glaring at me, "You making threats?" he said.

I shook my head in disapproval, then I leaned in and put my hand on the left side of my mouth like I was trying to tell a secret. The man's eyes widened, and he leaned in to hear me.

I whispered, "Not making threats, just making you aware of them. You've heard of the 'Droolin'-Dalton Gang', right?"

He nodded his head, his eyebrows knitting together in a worried expression.

We both turned to look at Bosun, he had gotten bored of the pocket knives and had found the biggest serrated machete on display. He was gripping it firmly, a serious look on his face, as he slowly practiced bringing the machete above his head and then slashing it down. The calm, slow movements and the muscles bulging from under his fur, made the almost meditative look on his face all the more menacing.

The salesman's brow was starting to perspire, his eyes transfixed on the blade in Bosun's hands.

I continued to whisper, "The gang had something important to them stolen by a lizard hyped up on your product and as much I want to keep them calm, they're looking for blood. They know you sell it and they intend to get answers, one way or another."

The man's eyes bulged, as he stared at Bosun. The canine was examining the blade and tested the sharpness with his thumb, sensing eyes on him he turned to look at us. The man's face snapped towards me to avoid eye contact with my companion, he looked like he was about ready to jump out of his own skin.

The man let out a gravely nervous cough, "I have no control over what they do on my product." He whispered.

"I get it, I totally understand. These gangsters though... well, you know what they're like." I pointed at my bruised face.

His eyes flickered back to Bosun, who was now in the tools section. He was playing around with a large cordless power drill, pulling the trigger, smiling as the thing spun and whirred loudly. Bosun nodded his head thoughtfully.

The slimy pawnbroker was pale as a ghost, no doubt reconsidering his path in life.

"My most recent sale was a reptile that goes by Pennon." He said breathlessly.

"Can you describe him for me?" I said.

"Dark blue scales, almost black. Light blue speckles on the face. Really built, had a physique that made me wonder why he needed the pheromones to begin with." He said, his face looking clammy.

Placing my hands flat on the counter, I leaned in closer. "And how do I find him?" I asked.

He grabbed a mustard stained napkin that was residing behind the counter and started frantically scribbling onto it.

Then pushing it towards me, while glancing at my friend again he asked "Settled?"

"Square," I replied, picking up the napkin and stuffing it into my pocket.

I snapped my fingers, remembering another question. "Almost forgot, does the name Gordon Baron ring a bell?" I queried.

The man scratched his nose, "I don't think so," he looked upwards searching his memory, "Haven't heard of him, why?" He grimaced, clearly believing not knowing the name could cause Bosun to retaliate.

"Don't worry about it" I said.

His teeth chattered as he said "This won't come back to me right?"

I smiled, "Of course not"

I turned to towards the exit, looked at Bosun and caught his eyes. Nodding towards the door I began to walk, Bosun looked at the pawnbroker and set the drill down. The salesman must have been holding his breath, because as Bosun and I strode out the door I heard a loud sigh of relief.

Walking towards the car I patted Bosun on the back saying, "Good job catching on to my plan."

Bosun's brow furrowed in confusion, "Catching what?" he asked.

I stopped, looking back towards the shop, then facing Bosun again, "The intimidation?" I imitated playing with an electric drill.

Bosun froze for a second, registering my words, confusion still written all over his face. It seemed to click in his head "O' Course," he said, quickly shifting his eyes from side to side "Yer welcome."

I had to stifle a laugh as I opened the car door. "Now to find this Pennon." I said.

"Is Gordon with the guy?" Bosun said as his ears perked up expectantly.

I stepped into the driver's seat, "Not sure, but he'll likely know where we can look." I said.

"After ya get the engine, yer not gonna run off are ya?" Bosun sat in the passenger's seat, clasping his hands together nervously.

I thought about it for a moment. Bosun clearly had all the downsides of being a canine xenoform; short attention span, low intelligence, and hyperactivity. But that meant he probably had all the upsides, too—and his devotion to his brother certainly showed his tendency towards loyalty. I didn't know what I'd gotten myself into, but having a loyal, hulking beast who could swing a machete following me around gave me a sense of comfort.,

I looked at him. "If you agree to have my back, I'll have yours." I said, keeping my terms simple and direct.

Bosun's anxiety instantly melted away, his tail violently wagging as he began to pant happily. "Dont'cha worry none. I'll bop that snake fer ya." he said, shaking his fists excitedly.

I chuckled and started the car.

...

Driving down secluded streets with Bosun tilting his head out of the open passenger side window, I considered our situation. The address on the greasy napkin said that Pennon resided in Warehouse 114 in the Harbor District. I felt a lot safer with Bosun, but that didn't change the fact that this was dangerous. There was no guarantee that was Pennon was alone or even still residing in that "Vacant" warehouse.

Hylathans are slippery shapeshifters and Pennon was likely one of many criminal aliases. Tracking him down if he wasn't where we were headed... I didn't like to think about how cold this case might get. Without Pennon I had no idea where we could look for either the engine or Gordon. I glanced at my new friend beside me.

"Bosun, listen here." I said.

He closed the window, looking at me while his tongue lazily hung from his mouth.

"This 'sketchy' job your brother was on, what was it exactly?" I asked.

His forehead furrowed, he looked to be thinking hard. "He said it was another test subject job. Ya know, when they try new techs on somebody fer cash?"

"A clinical trial?" I asked.

He nodded his head, "Yah," he grimaced, "Gordon, he was born with a club foot. He got some tech implants, fixin' it when we was kids"

I raised an eyebrow, "Okay?" I slowly said, confused as to what the Bosun's point was.

He scratched at his neck and continued, "When they was testing how his body would take it, they figured he was special." He glanced at me, "Ya get how those techs work, right?" he asked.

I caught on and nodded, "Everyone has different thresholds. Cybernetic implants not only take a toll on the body; but also the mind" I said.

Bosun nodded approvingly, his tail wagging slightly, he seemed glad I was understanding.

"Techs and mutations, Gordon can handle lots. So people ask him to test stuff." he said.

"I'm guessing that the kind of burden that would make most catatonic, he can bear?" I asked.

Bosun smiled, "Yah, he's tough like that" he said.

"Did he tell you where the trial was?" I asked.

The dog head drooped sadly in response, "Yah. First place I looked, building were deserted. I could smell him and that lizard, I couldn't track em' from there. That's when I got that taxi and started sniffing for anything."

"I see. If all else fails, we'll check out that building. I may find something." I said.

The blackboxon my belt vibrated. I instinctively started reaching for it when large clawed finger entered into my periphery. Distracted from Jean's call, I looked at Bosun.

He was pointing at a road ahead, "The warehouse is down that street," he started cracking his knuckles, "Gonna thump that snake" he said.

Turning the steering wheel, I said "Let's hope that we don't need to." I felt a pang of guilt think about Jean, she will have to wait.

We slowed down, trying to spot 'Warehouse 114'. Scanning my eyes from dilapidated warehouse to dilapidated warehouse, I spotted old gang graffiti and broken windows.

"Hundred twelve, hundred thirteen, there we go." I said, pulling into the warehouse parking lot.

We stepped out of the car and closed the doors. "One moment, Bosun" I said.

He glanced at me curiously, as I took out my

experi-sense kit. "For security." I said, affixing the camera to my glasses.

After the kit was all in place, I clicked record on the Black Box. "Surprise, you're on camera" I chuckled.

Bosun shot me a self-assured smile and a thumbs up. As confident as I was portraying myself to be, I worried about the likelihood of a fight. This Pennon guy was a heavy hitter without the aid of pheromones, I glanced at Bosun; I regretted not picking up at least a taser at the pawnshop.

I wasn't sure how much I could fight, considering my earlier injuries. Not to say I'm a fighter to begin with; even in perfect health I've never been skilled in self-defense.

Bland, concrete warehouse 114 stood before me, the front was lined with closed trailer drop-off bays and one employee door. The Parking lot was full of cracks, little weeds were growing in between them, seemingly the only signs of life in this area. I turned to Bosun.

"Be careful, ready for anything" I said.

Bosun rolled his shoulders and stretched his neck side to side, "Okay" he said.

"We move slow and quiet, if there are people in there we leave and make a new plan. First try negotiation, get him to willingly give us what we need." I said.

He nodded, a determined look on his face.

I nodded back and we started approaching the employee door.

Walking up the outside stairs to the door, I slowly turned the handle. Cautiously opening the door to peek in. It was dim inside, but the dusty windows let in just enough light to see the large sorting machines, conveyor belts, boxes and pallets silhouetted. Glancing around the inner door frame for anything suspicious, I stepped in and Bosun followed.

Gently closing the door with a muffled click, Bosun turned around and started sniffing the air. His nose twitching, his ears perking up. A distraught expression came over his face, as he glanced at me and motioned to follow him with his right hand.

"What?" I whispered.

He put his finger to his mouth, telling me to be quiet. "Blood" he murmured.

Cold unease knotted up in my stomach, I stepped closer to one of the large shipping crates beside me. I hoped that the shadows of the crates would hide my presence from any looming threat.

Bosun crouched low, kept moving and glancing around. His ears were high with alert and I could see the glint of his teeth exposed by his snarled expression. He stopped, looking down at something behind the crate at the end of the line. He waved me over and I quickly stepped over to him, my heart beating like a race-horse's.

Looking behind the crate, I saw it was an oil-covered rag. I peered at Bosun, my eyebrow raised. He glowered back at me, upset that I didn't understand him. He slowly bent down, picking up the rag out of the shadows and held it in the dim light.

My heart skipped as the black oil was revealed to be reddish-brown dried blood. My breath caught, I stepped back and placed my hand on the closest crate to keep balance. Doing my best to not hyperventilate, I nodded to Bosun.

Giving me a sidelong glance, he dropped the rag. Continuing on, he approached one of the machines and peered suspiciously around it. After gaining back some of my composure, I stealthily stepped forward. Bosun continued around the machine and out of my line of view.

Shit, I thought as I picked up the pace to catch-up to my friend. Quickly making my way beside the machine and turning the corner.

My foot struck something hard. Something metal clanged, clattered and skittered loudly across the floor, sending my nerves into overdrive. I looked about and saw a metal toolbox on the floor next to the machine. If only I had rounded the corner less sharply...

I stayed frozen in place, waiting for some response to my blunder. Bosun looked over his shoulder at me, wide eyed and shocked, still crouching.

We both stood stiff with fear for a long moment, straining our ears to hear if we alerted anyone. In the dim light our statuesque silhouettes waited, in between each stressful second we shifted our eyes trying to catch whatever may have been lurking in the shadows. We held our breath, breathing only as deeply as we dared.

Several moments passed like this, with us stuck in the dark silence that threatened us. Finally, seeming to gain back his confidence, Bosun straightened up standing at his full height. He seemed to relax, until his nose started violently twitching again. He growled, low and gravely, his stature became more imposing as his hair stood on end.

Fangs shining wet with saliva, his face contorted with rage. He continued his menacing sounds, directed at whatever malicious force that was watching us. I couldn't decide what I feared more, Bosun in this moment or whatever was hidden unseen.

My thoughts went back to the toolbox, I looked at the ground. I could make out the tools basic shapes laying scattered across the floor. I bent down slowly and soundlessly picked up a large monkey wrench. I held it firmly in my right hand, the weight of it made me feel only slightly less terrified.

A repetitive click-clacking echoed through the building, the noise bouncing off of the walls and making it difficult to determine its origin. It was getting louder, my blood went cold; it was getting closer. My mind flashed back to Glenmont's safe, the sound was the claws on his feet!

"Pennon!" I yelled, but it was too late for negotiation.

Suddenly, from out the darkness, a large Hylathan flung himself to flank Bosun. Bosun side-stepped, and the draconic figure's clawed hand tore through the air and luckily not the canine's flesh Bosun's leg lashed out at the scaled attacker, connecting solidly with the side of his left knee. The Hylathan shrieked, clawing forward and grazing Bosun's nose with the tips of his claws.

Bosun yelped in response, his nose spurting blood. Pennon launched another strike, ripping into Bosun's shirt as the canine backed away. I trembled, attempting to convince my legs to move. The big

Hylathan's razor-sharp clawed hand raised up to slash at my companion again, and I chucked the wrench in my hand at our attacker's head.

The tool slammed into the side of the lizard's face with a bone-reverberating thud. The wrench clattered to the floor, and the draconian figure's footing faltered. He turned his saw-toothed mouth in my direction and angrily hissed. He took a step towards me, his eyes like a shark's filled with murder.

That moment of distraction was all Bosun needed, though. The big dog tackled the Hylathan, wrapping him up in a bear hug and wrestling him to the floor. They squirmed and bit into each other, hissing and snarling like a pair of demon-possessed feuding cats. I ran to a stack of nearby wooden pallets as they fought for dominance. The Hylathan was slowly grappling his way on top of Bosun; I grabbed one of the wooden pallets.

The Hylathan gained the upper hand, straddling Bosun and snapping at his neck. The struggling dog tried his best to hold his attacker off. I sprinted towards them and swung the pallet down with all my weight squarely onto the draconic man's back.

The Hylathan screamed a blood-curdling scream, his torso arching backwards as if in horrendous pain. I hadn't seen that coming—I'd expected a moment of distraction, or maybe to put him off-balance with the assault, but the Hylathan writhed in apparent agony. He fell onto his side, off of Bosun, and grasped at his back, still curling like he was trying to fold his spine in half. Wriggling like an ant on fire, the lizard-man continued to shriek with tears in his eyes.

Bosun scrambled up, bloody, breathing heavily, and delivered a swift, massive kick to the scaled figure's head, which cut the screaming short as the Hylathan blanked into unconsciousness..

I put my hand on Bosun's shoulder, he whipped around to face me, still snarling for a moment. He blinked as he saw me, relaxing his shoulders and stepping away from the unconscious humanoid lizard.

The Hylathan lay face-down, sprawled across the floor. His cheap, blue sweatpants were accentuated with splotches of blood. I looked at his head, a small pool of red liquid was collecting around it; Bosun must have knocked out a couple of his fangs.

Blood stained strips of fabric caught my eye as I scanned his back. A nagging feeling tugged at my brain, something about this scene wasn't right. I looked at Bosun leaning against a crate, I snapped my eyes back to the Hylathan and my jaw dropped.

Makeshift bandages. I peeled back one of the soaked, sticky strips gagging with disgust and horror. The way he squirmed when I hit his back made perfect sense to me, now.

His wings had been hacked clean off, leaving a wretched, useless, exposed nub on each shoulder.

FOUR

I FRANTICALLY PACED BACK and forth across the dusty concrete warehouse floor. Bosun had lifted the Hylathan into a folding chair and was tying him into place with a grungy old rope. We stood in a backroom, surrounded by packed boxes of personal items. A disheveled mattress lay on the floor in the far corner, and clothing littered the floor. This room must have housed the lizard-man for at least a few weeks.

I had cautiously checked the rest of the warehouse, making sure that we were the only three souls in the building. In the back loading bay, covered with tarps except for the open on-ramp that our suspect had been loading boxes into, a small ship with just enough amenities for two to three people if they wanted to get really cozy awaited anyone who wanted to leave the planet very, very suddenly.

Still nervously pacing, I thought over the situation in my head. I looked to the hylathan's slumping body—how long would it take for him to wake up? We needed answers.

Besides which, the amputation of his wings struck me as a grievous cruelty. I knew, just from the layout of the thing, that his wings had to have been present during the robbery. That meant whoever now had the Engine had also likely caused the gruesome state of his back.

I glanced at Bosun. How exactly did his brother play into this? I had to wonder whether this Gordon character, was an innocent in this matter. Knowing how emotional Bosun is, I would never dare discuss with him this dark possibility, that his beloved brother might be capable of causing such pain.

Bosun finished tying up the Hylathan, then knelt in front of the lizard and lifted one of our captive's eyelids. The iris was a startlingly bright yellow color, like sticky amber that could entrap you for eternity. He waved his finger from left to right in front of his unmoving eye, checking for consciousness. If the Hylathan was faking, then he was a pro.

I watched as Bosun gently shook him, and when that did nothing he lightly slapped him a few times across his snout. The Hylathan didn't move a muscle, and my friend sighed.

"Ya' don't wake soon, I'll douse ya' in machine oil buddy" the canine threatened.

Remembering the experi-sense kit still set up on me, I considered putting it away when my phone rang in my jacket pocket. Not wanting to answer right now, I clicked the hang-up button without looking at the phone. A few seconds past by and it started ringing obnoxiously again, I pulled it from my pocket, checked the caller ID and then put it to my ear.

I answered, "Sylvester, this isn't the best tim-"

On the other end Sylvester interrupted me, "*What have you done*, Martin?!" he asked with his high-pitched voice wavering between anger and fear.

Bosun's ears shot up in response to the panic he could hear from the phone. He slowly turned to face me, as his hair bristled.

I scowled saying, "Syl, calm down. I don't under-"

"You know damn well what I'm asking!" He yelled.

"No Syl, I don't" I said.

"You've gone crazy, I shoulda' known from how you been actin'. This ain't right Martin, this ain't right!" Sylvester said, huffing exasperatedly.

I felt a lump in my throat; ready to burst as my mind struggled to keep up with my lounge-singer friend's panic.

"You... I..." Sylvester gasped for breath, "I'd never let this happen if I knew you would-" He stopped himself short, still gasping for air.

"You're running yourself ragged, Syl. Please, calm yourself. Try to breathe," I said as neutrally as I could. Even as I kept my voice level, the beginnings of a panic attack encroached on me.

"This is how much I'm worth, huh? Everything I done for you, and this is what you do?" Sylvester sharply whispered, "Just murder the bastard I lead you to?"

A cold shock ran down my spine and Bosun visibly stiffened, his eyes widening. Maybe this was a coincidence, I thought to myself. That pawn shop wasn't exactly in the best area, nor did it have the best clientele. Maybe it wasn't somebody trying to clean up loose ends. Maybe they weren't after the loose end we had tied to this chair in front of us.

Maybe. But probably not.

Sylvester's voice pitched higher as he cried. "How dare you make me party to this, Martin?"

"I swear I haven't killed anyone Syl," I pleaded.

"What the hell is going on then!?" He screamed at me.

I heard a low chuckling from behind Bosun. The Hylathan's eyes flickered open and closed. He still slumped forward exhausted, but a slowly forming smile began to reveal his blood-slicked fangs. Bosun whipped around to face the Hylathan, his hands balled into fists.

"Knew I shoulda' been more careful," the lizard's voice caught as he began a coughing fit.

"Martin! Answer me!" Sylvester on the other end yelled.

Bosun grabbed the Hylathan's shoulders and shook him, "Where's Gordon? Speak or I'll-"

The lizard-man interrupted Bosun in a low, hissing voice. "Gave the dealer this address, rookie move. That's what I get for gettin' excited." He laughed, then coughed again. "So excited, I didn't check who was really callin' the shots."

"Syl, listen. I'm no killer. I'm only guilty of biting off more than I can chew. For your own safety go to Dr. Glenmont's estate, and yes 'The Dr. Glenmont.' Tell him I sent you, that you need protection. I don't know what I'm up against here, but this is much bigger than I thought. Stay put, and stay safe," I said, and pulled the phone away from my ear.

As I did, I heard the sound of clattering metal—the same sound as when I kicked the tool box earlier. Bosun and I froze, glancing at one another. With a click, I hung up the phone and slipped it away.

The canine's nose twitched and his ears drew back, a low growl emanating from his snarling mouth.

"The party followed me here, huh?" the hylathan whispered with a crooked smile. "The boys weren't content with leavin' me in this state,"

I had no idea how many there were and how heavily armed, but "more than us" was probably a safe bet on either count. That made our first priority getting the hell out of there. The memory of the tarp-covered ship flashed in my mind's eye. I turned and sprinted towards the backroom hallway.

Bosun's eyes widened in panic, looking from the bedroom door the enemy was likely to arrive through and to the direction I was running. I ran past him as loud, thudding footsteps approached the bedroom door.

To his credit, the big canine xenoform grabbed the back of the chair with our hylathan captive and followed me. As he dragged the snarling lizard-man through the door into the backroom, I saw the several black-clad, well-armed men running after us. I turned back around and ran up the ship's ramp.

"Hold it!" yelled one of our black-clad pursuers.

Once inside the ship its bright, flourescent lights automatically lit up for me. The outdated vessel creaked as I ran to sit behind the driver's panel – exactly the sort of sound one does not want to hear from the thing about to stand between one and hard vacuum. A large, blue tarp still obscured the front windshield. I fumbled to find the engine start.

Scanning my eyes from button to button, lever to lever, I heard a gunshot ring out. The sound of the blast bounced between the walls of the hull and my ears rang. Frantically, I began to flip random switches, desperately hoping one would be my salvation.

With one switch the windshield wipers flung themselves helplessly at the tarp, with another the spotlights on the outside flashed brilliantly enough for the light to pass through the tarp, I grasped a knob and it opened a panel door near my feet to reveal a canned-beer-filled mini fridge.

I turned to see Bosun dragging a still-tied-and-struggling hylathan up the ship's ramp. The lizard arched his head back to look towards me, he was snarling fiercely. With a small bending of the knees and a slight winding back, the dog harshly chucked his captive in my direction. The lizard flew through the air momentarily, then crashed to the floor next to my feet, his chair shattering with a loud crack and his eyes rolling back in his head once more.

"The bright green switch!" Bosun yelled.

Outside, our pursuer's heavy footfalls approached outside of my view.

I looked back to the driver's panel, flicking my eyes from left to right hoping to find the green switch.

I peered behind me. The on-ramp was still open, and through it, out the back of the ship, I could see the loading dock behind us slowly getting farther away. Bosun was barely inside the ship, he looked from the ramp to me and nodded, then spun behind the wall as a couple more gunshots rang out.

I returned my attention to the panel, trying to find the green switch. My heart raced, and I tried to focus my mind on finding our salvation in the forest of small little toggles. At last, I found it, a pale, sickly, and at the moment, beautifully green toggle. My hand flew up and flipped it, and the rumbling sound of engines beginning to spool up greeted me. The deckplates of the ship vibrated with its building power.

I heard footfalls on the ramp. One of the men entered, and I got my first look at them. The black outfit screamed private military of some sort. The armored vest had a number of pockets, black kneepads, and a black baseball cap turned backwards completed the ensemble. The man trained his gun on Bosun, but looked away from me as he did. I reflexively reached into the mini fridge below the driver's panel and wrapped my hand around a cold one, then stood, spun, and hurled the heavy can with a cry and all my strength.

The turned to me. Bosun lifted his head and tracked the trajectory of the drink. Time seemed to slow as the can of cheap beer arced through the air, then made impact with the man's chest.

The can burst and beer foam sprayed in all directions. The entirety of onlookers paused for a moment, watching the spectacle; Bosun moved first, taking the opportunity to grab the man by his vest collar, then casually slamming him into the side of the ship. The ramp outside snapped shut, presumably part of the launch sequence the green switch had triggered. Further bullets clanged against the hull, but with the hatch closed our intruder had been cut off from his support. He slumped to the floor as Bosun casually relieved him of his assault rifle, then looked up at me with a proud, goofy expression that only made sense on his canine face.

Then the ship lurched, and Bosun fell to the deckplates as the engines finally went from spooling up to firing. I staggered, but pressed my hand against the ceiling's roof to stabilize myself, then turned back around to look at the windshield as the tarp blew away, revealing our speedy approach towards the windowed ceiling.

I slammed my eyelids shut, and my whole body tensed. The ship shook with the impact and the engine whirred its angry disapproval. Crashing and clinking of breaking glass and the metallic tearing of steel frames tore across the outside of the hull. This was all followed by the sound of rushing wind and whimpers of our intruder.

I slowly opened my eyes. The clear night sky was apparent through the windshield and our hylathan was at the controls smirking at me. I turned my head towards Bosun, who was now wrenching the arm of the man behind his back. The outfitted mercenary cried out quietly in pain, he was no longer fighting back.

Bosun still panting, dragged the intruder to the back left corner of the hull, the man cried out "Stop! Stop! Please" as he kicked at the floor.

The canine shoved him into the corner

slamming the man's back against the intersecting walls and angrily shouted, "Stay!" He pointed his index finger at the floor in a jerking motion.

The man nodded, his face was pale and compared to his previous companions he was shorter and thinner. His eyes were a dark lifeless brown, surrounded by greyish skin around them, a tell-tale sign of lack of sleep. As Bosun patted down and searched the many pockets of the intruder, I noticed how young this man looked. His face was weary, but still smooth and elastic, he couldn't be older than twenty one.

I heard a few clicks behind me and I looked to see the hylathan setting up what had to be autopilot, then he turned to face us.

"Just now, you were screamin' for him to stop," he said in a mocking tone at the man, a fanged sneer forming across his muzzle. "Earlier today," he paused dramatically "I remember sayin' the same thing"

The hylathan looked back, as if to peer at the ghost of his wings. Then he turned back shrugging non-nonchalantly, but his eyes maintained their piercing, predatory stare. The ship's cabin lights had turned his amber eyes into a color closer to fiery magma; they seemed to burn into the very soul of our would-be assailant.

The young man's beer-soaked, messy, tree-bark brown hair clung to his pale and terrified face. His gaze did not leave the Hylathan's dangerous stare. His hands shook at his sides, as Bosun finished searching him and removed a knife and stun gun from his pockets.

Bosun tossed me the stun gun, I reached out

and caught it. The dog glanced at the hylathan, then at me; the message was less than subtle.

The hylathan rolled his eyes and crossed his arms across his chest. "I'm in piss poor state for fightin'," he said. "And it seems as you want information, and my former employers want to kill me. Given my druthers, I'd choose to be interrogated over killed. Let's start with this: my name is Pennon. I'm a thief. Recently, I took a job—and found out afterwards who had hired me. The same people that hired this man, I'd wager. The sons of Balil. And if I had to guess...this here is a mercenary who's also been hired by them. Is that about what you were looking to know?"

I drew my breath in sharply. The sons—more of a race, now, than an organization. Cruel, enslaving, body-snatchers. The sons of Balil are Manzala's boogeyman, a species of world-conquering body snatchers. A race of corrupt monstrosities, that when faced with low fertility decided upon pseudo-immortality, forcing their souls into the bodies of others and creating amalgamated creatures to inhabit.

I shuddered; this mercenary hadn't imagined the possibility that his troop could be hired by these avatars of rotten flesh imbued with necrotic science, meshed with electronic nightmares of cybernetics gone too far. People didn't like to think of such grotesque things, so they didn't. The conflict between Manzala and The sons Of Balil had become a cold war, a conflict too distant from everyday life of citizens to care.

Manzala was a city open to everyone, and

everything—but the sons wanted it. Wanted the gateways. Wanted the stranglehold over trade that control of the city would bring. And wanted the access to other worlds, to collect the genetic material of as many races as they could, constantly updating themselves into more powerful monsters. And that—that's who I'd picked a fight with.

I should have charged extra.

Boson, however, shrugged off this revelation and turned back to his captive. He leaned in, bringing his face level with the man's, the mercenary's eyes flitted to Bosun's.

"Where's my brother?" he asked.

The young man shot me a confused glance like I could help him, I ignored his pleading look and with some difficulty stood up, then walked over to the small red bench pushed up against the left wall. I sat down, now that guns weren't going off I could actually look at my surroundings.

The hull was the size of an average studio apartment, with two bunk beds built into the wall across from me, the side I was sitting on was lined with benches and cabinets. There was a door near the right corner by the ramp, I assume it's the bathroom. The color scheme of the whole ship is red and silver, I glanced at Pennon. The contrast between his blue and the red around him felt jarring, like squinting too intensely at an old-school 3D drawing, hoping that if you try hard enough you'll make the image pop on your own.

A blaring migraine began to form behind my forehead, I looked down, placing my face into my hands and closed my eyes.

I heard Bosun continue, "Gordon Baron, where's he?"

The man could only stammer incoherently, I then heard Bosun growl and what sounded like him violently shaking the man.

I sighed, lifted my head up, stood and walked over to the two of them. Putting a hand on the canine's shoulder, he stopped shaking the guy and looked at me, his ears flattened back.

"We know Pennon stole the Dwarven Engine," I jutted my thumb behind me towards the Hylathan, "We know that Gordon picked up Pennon's scent today, before disappearing" I said.

"Wait, lanky kid with a bunch of implants?" Pennon asked.

Bosun's ears perked up as he turned to face the speaker, "Yah! Where's he?" he asked.

Pennon's face darkened, "Was pickin' up my pay at this pop-up clinic, saw him in the waitin' room" he said.

"And?" Bosun prodded.

Pennon shook his head, "He was leavin' as I got there. Got called into a room, the fuckers strapped me to a table and..." he clenched his jaw and shut his eyes.

"How did you get out?" I asked.

He clenched his fists, then after a moment let himself relax, "They'd just finished clippin' me, when they got called to help with somethin'. Sounded like someone was fightin' back. Them leavin' gave me the chance to cut the straps and book it—can't say I paid attention to much else past that." he replied.

Bosun scowled, "But ya' don't know what happened to my brother?" he said.

Pennon shook his head again, "Who knows with makeshift clinics like that?" he said and shrugged.

The dog's ears drooped down in disappointment, then slowly slicked back as a low growl emanated from his chest. He glowered at the terrified young man, his lips pulling back to reveal his pointed canines. The man's chest rose and fell in a frantic pace, he was hyperventilating.

With one monstrous paw my companion wrapped his fingers around the mercenary's throat. The man let out a small squeak as Bosun's grip tightened.

I stepped forward, a pang of fear for the youngster's life struck me. "Bosun." I said, trying to keep my voice calm and soothing.

Bosun was stock still, "Won't kill 'em" he said.

My fingers clenched down on the stun gun, I desperately hoped he was telling the truth.

"Don't know who sons o' Ballet are, but when I find Gordon and I come to figure ya' hurt em'... I'll eat yer eyeballs." he growled menacingly.

The man pressed his back against the wall harder, a useless attempt to distance himself from my companion.

"They're gonna kill me if I say a word." the man said, his pallid face was dripping with sweat.

"Then yer stuck between a rock and the things I'll do to yah if yah don't," Bosun said, as he tightened his grip on the man's throat.

The mercenary gulped, his eyes open wide with

horror were almost the size of silver dollars. As terrible as he is, I can't help but empathize. The sons...failing them could lead to something far worse than death.

The labored breathing of the man as Bosun squeezed his neck, snapped me out of my inner thoughts.

Wheezing the man said, "If I'd known what I'd be doing I-",

Pennon interrupted him with a sneer, "You have no problem with doin' this kinda shit," He pointed to his injured back, "Your problem is findin' out who hired you."

Pennon slinked a few steps closer, "Cowardly bastards like you are gung-ho to ruin lives, at least until you find out how ready your employer is to ruin yours," he said.

"Hypocrite," I muttered under my breath, I started grinding my teeth.

Pennon's head snapped to face me, his blazing eyes locking onto me. "What was that?" he hissed.

I fought my deepest instincts to cower away and met his eyes with mine, "Hypocrite," I clenched down on the stun gun in my hand again, "You're just as guilty."

Pennon glowered at me with those predatory lava-like eyes, his clawed feet clinked against the metal floor as he tapped them in frustration.

"I don't chop off people's body parts," Pennon hissed.

Bosun turned to scowl at Pennon, "Not fer a lack of tryin'," he said as he pointed at the gash on his nose.

The lizard clenched his fists, "You would've done the same if you were bein' hounded by these bastards," he huffed and threw out a hand to motion towards the frightened mercenary.

"And what about the engine?" I asked.

"What of it, old man?" Pennon said in a petulant tone.

The corners of my mouth came up in a mocking smirk, "You were pretty gung-ho about stealing it," I said.

Pennon stomped his foot, "I wouldn't have if I-"

"If yah knew who yah was working fer?" Bosun interrupted flatly.

The lizard opened his mouth to respond, but thought better of it. He pressed his lips into a firm line and turned away from us, opting to look nonchalantly at the driver's panel instead of the three passengers behind him.

I shook my head and loosened my fingers around the stun gun, I need to focus on getting answers. I glanced back at the young mercenary and squatted down beside Bosun, flitting my eyes from the wan shaking face of our captive, to his pockets.

"You took all his belongings, right Bosun?" I asked.

"Just his weapons," the canine replied.

Pennon clicked his tongue and sighed in a dramatic fashion.

Bosun's lips pulled back to reveal his fangs, "Problem, Snake?" he questioned Pennon.

The lizard shrugged his shoulders exaggeratedly, "Nothing, I just shouldn't be surprised that a dog built as thick as bricks," he waved his right hand in a flourish around his right ear, "would be just as smart as a concrete slab," he said in an annoyed sarcastic tone.

Bosun's ears drooped down, a tired and annoyed look across his face. His eyes flickered to me, eyebrows raised expectantly.

After a quick moment I nodded and said, "I was wondering if he had any electronics."

The mercenary, still firmly attached by the throat to Bosun's imposing hand, squirmed at the mention of tech. Bosun's focus shot back to the man, he tightened his grip and with the other hand sifted through the pockets again.

A few loose coins clattered against the floor, then a pen, a wallet, a credit stick, and finally a cellphone was removed from his pockets.

I picked up the cellphone and turned it on. The bright screen lit up to reveal a request for a password, I showed the locked screen to the man.

"I won't," the mercenary said breathlessly.

"You don't have to, it would just make things easier," I said, with a forced smile camouflaging my discomfort.

I walked back to the red bench and sat down, then I pulled out my netbook, opened it up, whipped out a connection cord and snapped the ends of the wire into the phone and computer.

"I hate to brute force your code, but you have to admit it's better than having the answers strangled from you by my friend." I said trying to lighten the mood, I leisurely tapped at my keyboard.

When I said I hate to do this, I was lying through my teeth. I'm too nosy of a person to not get a kick from my job, finding items and figuring out what happened to said items is my jam. Algorithms and a little snooping, my bread and butter.

My lips twitched upwards into a smile, as I prepared the software to in a matter of seconds guess every possible password. It wasn't an elegant solution, but it got me what I wanted; results. I glanced at the man, still soaked with beer and dread, then with a light click I pressed 'Enter' and the computer's processor silently whirred through every combination of letters and numbers conceivable.

A sigh of relief escaped my lips, with technology violence wasn't necessary and answers could be derived without knocking someone's teeth out. My head throbbed for a moment and I glanced at Bosun, as much as I appreciate his help, I dislike his use of physical force. I shifted a little on the bench and felt the shape of the Black Box in my pocket. I realized I was still wearing my Exper-Sense kit, but no longer cared enough to put it away.

I froze for a moment reminded of Jean and thought to myself *'with the press of a button, every problem can be solved.'*

A light ding reverberated around the hull from my computer's speakers, telling me its task was done. I unplugged the phone from my computer and packed the netbook back into my jacket pocket. Flicking my thumb across the screen, I began my search through the mercenary's files. He had some new messages from his associates demanding his status and location, those were going to be ignored.

I flipped though his memos, a random list of

songs, a short shopping list and finally a note simply titled 'Job'.

Job
Wellish Clinic, Warehouse 97, Hayer Street
8:40AM Tester interviews
9AM Engine Booster pick up
1:30PM Tester pick ups
47°S, 13°W Altay

Not looking away from the phone I asked, "Pennon, the name of the clinic?"

"Wellish, or some shit," the lizard said, then shrugged.

I could see Bosun in my peripherals, his ears went up in alert and his shoulders tensed. "Wellish was were he said he were going," he whispered.

Tearing my eyes from the phone screen, I turned my gaze to the mercenary. He was still being held in place by the large canine, and he gave me a pitiful defeated look.

I held up the phone and pointed to it, "So the engine and Gordon, your friends took them to Altay,"

The man's eyes bulged in shock, as a low growl came from Bosun and I wondered how much of the mercenary's expression was the fault of strangulation.

Pennon's jaw was agape, "That shit, canyon ridden, mining planet? You were going to chop me up and ship me there!" he said.

Bosun scowled angrily, "Why's he there?" he said, staring daggers at the young captive.

The mercenary stammered in response, "We were only hired to collect what they wanted and deliver,"

"Like you don't have any idea whatsoever," Pennon sneered, "It's not like you're working for a bunch of twisted body-snatchers or anythin'!" he sarcastically waved his hands.

Suddenly Bosun picked up the young man and held him in the air, the monstrous dog snarled and foamed from the mouth. The man gasped for air and clawed at the hands around his neck, kicking his legs frantically.

"Body-snatchin'? Where's Gordon!" Bosun roared.

Pennon jeered, "Maybe the coward ain't talkin' cause he cut him up, just like they were doin' to me," the lizard took several steps closer to Bosun, leaning in to chide the mercenary "That's the truth, ain't it?"

Bosun's face turned into pure rage, his lips peeling as far back as they could go, his glistening fangs with foamed saliva clinging to them, his ears pressed back against his skull, and his eyes as dark and blind as black-holes ready to obliterate the man atom by atom.

I shot up from the bench, reaching for the stun gun I had been given earlier. "No!" I cried. "No killing!"

My companion's fury rendered him deaf and blind. His chest rumbled with a low growl that made my skin crawl, as it echoed around us. Pennon had an expression of anger as well, but his magma eyes shined with delight. Those haunting, burning eyes flitted to me and I realized the terrible position I was in.

Bosun was my only realistic protection and using the stun gun to stop him would make me vulnerable. If I didn't, our captive might die. A small smirk fell across the lizards lips. For him, this was win-win. For me...there was a decision to make.

FIVE

THE SHIP MOVED at a snail's pace, but that didn't stop my stomach from turning. My head ached, my eardrums throbbed and my heart felt like it was going to burst through my rib cage. Bosun was still strangling the mercenary. Moving in slow motion, the young man kicked and clawed at the enraged canine. Each strike becoming more lethargic as the lack of oxygen weakened him.

If I was in my companion's shoes, would I be willing to kill? Maybe... Maybe not. Missing brother or not, dead or alive, this was wrong. A blue tint began to spread across the man's face. Did Bosun even need Pennon egging him on to go this far? My gut did another somersault. Was all of this even worth the engine anymore? Worth the life of a stranger?

A visage of a gravestone hidden behind icy blue snow hung heavy in my mind, I clenched my teeth so hard my gums hurt. Salty tears welled in my eyes, threatening to roll down and sting at my scratched face. The nagging voice at the back of my skull called out to me, *'Coward'* it said.

Pennon, that slimy cretin, observed the struggle with a self-satisfied smile. His blazing eyes fixed on the two of them; I glanced at the mercenary's pistol still laying in a puddle on the floor. I clenched the stun gun and pocketed it. Before anyone could notice me, I jolted for the back of the ship.

I glanced back to see the lizard's gaze, flitting to me. His leg muscles tensed as he began stepping towards me, his hands up and open palmed in a faux-placating fashion. Only his fiery eyes gave away his malicious intent. Bosun's fury-filled face softened only slightly, as his shark-like eyes set upon me.

My already-frayed nerves burned with adrenaline and fear, I felt trapped in the lion's den. My shoes clapped across the wet, beer-covered surface and I quickly stooped, picking up the sopping wet gun. Drops of liquid dripped from the barrel as I swung it towards Pennon.

The lizard tried to halt, his talons skidding across the wet floor. His feet slipped forward and his body arched backwards, then he fell onto his back with a thud that only slightly shook the ship. Frozen in a wide fighting stance, my hands shook and my fingers desperately clung to the gun's handle, hoping the wet weapon wouldn't slide from my grasp.

Bosun, snapped out of his rage by the commotion, stared at the gun mouth agape.

My voice rattled through my chattering teeth, "Would your brother appreciate you killing in his name?"

The canine stood there for a moment in shock, then dropped the young man. The mercenary hit the floor, clambering weakly to his knees, gasping for air and clasping his throat with his hands. The bluish tint left his visage and his lungs stopped their erratic wheezing. The man began to sob, his every word unintelligible wailing gibberish.

Bosun's shocked expression faded, as he looked down at the mercenary. Ears slowly drooping down, jowls pulling up in disgust and narrowed crying eyes turning away from all of us. He rubbed his eyes and guiltily glanced at me, then the shaking gun, and finally to his own hands.

"Just want 'em back." the dog's voice broke, he gulped back more tears.

The voice in the back of my head still echoed. '*Coward.*' It had quieted some, now and I was determined to prove it wrong. The memory of the frozen cemetery tore at my brain, I focused on the heat of my anger in hopes of melting it away.

I steeled myself and forced my hands to stop shaking, "We will get him back," I said with as much resolve as I could muster.

The dog's eyes locked onto mine, wide with hope and still bright with lingering tears. His tail swayed in a slow wag.

"You're insane, cut your damn losses." Pennon said, his expression narrowing into a scowl.

I looked at the lizard, helplessly sprawled across the floor. "You just going to let them walk off with your wings?" I rebutted.

The Hylathan's frustrated expression only deepened, "Oh sure! Let's team up, buddy! With an introduction like this, we're sure to be the best of friends." he said, sarcasm practically dripping from his words.

"We are taking this ship to Altay, whether you are here to help or not." I said.

"I slaved away years for this for this ship." Pennon protested, worry in his eyes.

"No doubt you afforded this through robbing people blind," I said with a shrug. "Just look at us appropriating it as a form of redemption."

The lizard hissed, "You don't even know how to fly this thing." he clenched his fists and began to shake with anger.

"Bosun, start looking for an owner's manual." My furry friend nodded and began searching through cupboards. "I'm sure we will figure it out." I said to the ship's owner.

With that I strode over to the bench and sat down. Gun still in my hand, I kept it level with Pennon's chest, I glanced at the mercenary still huddled on the floor and pressed the frame of my glasses so they would sit more firmly on my face. My pocket vibrated.

Another pang of guilt struck me, Jean was calling again and I hadn't answered her in hours. My stomach clenched and the nagging part of myself scolded me, 'Selfish' it said. With my one empty hand I reached into my pocket and grasped the Black Box. My eyes flitted to Pennon's as I pulled the device out, one of the lizard's eyebrows raised in a questioning manner. I ignored him and brought the Black Box to my ear.

"Sorry for the radio silence, Jean." I said.

I could hear a sigh of relief on the other end, "I thought you'd never answer." she said.

Bosun walked over to me, some papers in his hands. Giving me a confused scowl, he held up the papers for me to glance at. He pointed at the first loose paper, trying to communicate non-verbally with me.

I squinted at the page, a diagram of the mini fridge was illustrated on it. "Sorry I made you worry," I shook my head at Bosun, "This case has been really hectic is all." I said.

Bosun turned the page towards himself, looked over it with a perplexed look, then shuffled through the papers and brought another page to my attention.

"Hectic like when you had to find that genetically modified raccoon?" she asked.

"Yah, the one that glowed in the dark and ate traffic cones. One of my very first cases, I chased that bugger all over the city." I chuckled.

Quickly looking over the paper my companion was trying to show me, I saw it listed the procedure on how to drain coolant from the vessel. We were going to have to sort through this bundle of loose papers that made up the manual, I sighed in frustration.

Jean's laugh rolled heartily out of the speaker, "You brought it home in a flimsy box, it was seething so much I thought it was going to end up loose in my kitchen for sure."

I chuckled at the memory and caught Pennon rolling his eyes. The mercenary knelt, his shoulders hunched and his head down, his breathing even and calm. Bosun just looked at me expectantly, his fingers crinkling the papers.

Bringing my attention back to Jean, I said "I got to get going, we will talk again soon enough."

"Okay, love you." she said.

"Ditto." I said and hung up.

Placing the device back in my pocket, I sighed and squeezed the bridge of my nose. "Can you hold the gun as I look over those papers?" I asked the waiting canine.

Bosun nodded and set the papers down on the bench next to me. I passed him the gun and he leaned into the wall behind him. Pressing his back firmly against the metal, he began to look over the pistol, absentmindedly running his thumb over the handle.

Picking up the papers, I scanned over the pages trying to pick out relevant information. They crinkled softly as I shuffled them in my hands. I had to wonder what happened to the manual's binding. I was glad to find that this ship was made for deep space, designed to camp out for long periods of time on asteroids. Altay is in the eleventh orbit of the system, hours away from our home planet Terradin —and that was before we figured in gaining clearance at an Altay Starport.

There are two Starports on Altay, one controlled by Ring-Miners and the other a clan of techno-dwarves. An idea struck me and I set down the jumbled manual next to me. Pulling out my phone, I started dialing Dr. Glenmont. The call didn't even get through the first ring before it was answered.

"Aten, is that you?" Glenmont hurriedly asked.

"Yes it's me, I was just calling to-" I was interrupted before I could finish.

"This is turning into an outright mess, a dead pawnbroker and you sent this Sylvester character to my home in a panic," he let out a long sigh, "He tells me you were saying something about the sons of Balil?"

"I've confirmed they stole your engine," I said and turned to look at the mercenary, "I'm certain they killed the broker," the young man's head whipped up in response to my words, his eyes were wide with panic.

"I- I didn't, it was my partner." the frightened man stammered.

Pennon rolled his eyes again, "Still party to it." he said.

I stared at the night sky glowing behind the ships windshield, "We also confirmed that Bosun's brother is involved. Gordon and the engine are likely on Altay." I said.

"And what basis do you draw this conclusion?" the techno-dwarf asked.

I bounced my right leg anxiously as I spoke, "Found coordinates on a mercenaries phone."

Glenmont was silent for a few seconds, "I feel I'm missing most of the context here." he said, a tinge of frustration in his voice.

"I'll start from where we last left off. After our video call in the car, Bosun and I visited the pawnbroker that had sold the pheromones to the thief. He gave us an address to a hylathan named Pennon, he was the one responsible for the robbery." I said.

In a demanding tone Glenmont said, "And where is the cretin now?"

My eyes flickered to the scaly criminal staring daggers back at me. He straightened his back and loudly said, "I'm right here."

I was taken aback; the lizard's hearing was far

more precise than mine. My stomach dropped, I realized the doctor most certainly heard him.

Another still moment passed and Glenmont said, "Hand him the phone, now."

Pennon reached out his hand, I didn't want to argue with my employer or the lizard, so I placed the device into his palm. I watched him bring the speaker to his ear.

"Hello, Monty," The thief said mockingly, a smile plastered on his lips.

I couldn't understand Dr. Glenmont's muffled response, but I could tell it was furiously gruff in tone.

The scaled one shook his head thoughtfully, "Can't get it back for you. If it makes you feel any better the sons didn't pay what they promised for it." he said, his sarcasm fading a little to show what seemed like a modicum of sincerity.

More muffled sounds came from the speaker, and Pennon listened intently. His eyes widened, and he let out a burst of laughter.

His shoulders shook as he chuckled, "Are you senile? I'm a 'cretin,' remember?"

I could hear a soft line of whispers coming out of the device. The lizard's laughter cut short as he pressed the phone harder against his cheek, burning focus in his eyes again.

He looked back at the empty space that used to be his wings, "I'm not in great shape for that, Doc," deliberating for only few seconds, he said slowly into the receiver, "Ever considered adoption?"

His fiery eyes flickered to me and then towards the wall in embarrassment. "My daughter, if you promised to give her your whole world..." he gulped nervously.

He clenched one of his fists, "Was gonna give her mine, after this job," he said, a deeply pensive look spreading across his features.

More seconds past and the lizard nodded as Glenmont spoke, the thief chuckled, "Yah, it's not much of a world to give."

His mouth curved into an even bigger smile, but his eyes grew darker and sad. "Good, I'll send her details. I'll get you back what I stole, I promise." he said.

Without even looking at me, Pennon tossed the phone to me. Playing hot potato for a moment between my hands, I managed to catch it and bring it to my ear. I said, "You still there?"

"Yes, so after your meeting with the pawnbroker?" Glenmont said nonchalantly.

"We located Pennon," I tapped my foot nervously, "Before we could have a real conversation with him, the sons mercenaries arrived." I looked at the still kneeling young man, "We managed to escape and take one of them with us. I searched his phone and found coordinates for Altay." I said.

"I'll help however I can from here, I'll use my credentials to get you through the techno – dwarf starport and head for the coordinates with a small team of my confidants." the inventor said.

"How will we-" I began to ask.

"They'll find you. With a rag tag group like yours, you'll be easy to spot." he said.

"Do you have any idea, what they are doing with my engine on Altay?" the dwarf asked.

"Not yet, I'll search his phone more thoroughly to see if I find anything." I replied.

"Send me the coordinates, I have some contacts I can question. If that is it I'll let you-" Glenmont said and was interrupted by Sylvester yelling in the background.

"Is Sylvester okay?" I asked.

"He wants to speak to you, hold on," he replied.

After a few moments of silence followed by ruffling sounds, Syl's sing-song voice was emitted from the phone. "I never thought you the type to become involved with the sons, but I should have known better, with the trouble you usually find yourself in and all."

"I'm really sorry Syl." I said.

"Don't be. I just need to ask one thing of you so if you meet Murphy's Law, it won't weigh on me." he said.

A few moments passed where I just listened intently, waiting for his question. A small sigh escaped the speaker and the singer continued, "You can quit. You know that, right? Jean, she wouldn't like this."

It felt like the floor dropped from underneath me, as I considered the possibility of giving up. I stood there, a sense of aimless floating all around me. The only gravity I could perceive was the beating mass in my chest, my heart pumping and pumping on. What were the consequences of my answer?

Panning my view from one side of the ship to the other, I stared at my company. Individual choices and individual consequences, at least that's what I'd like to think. What would my Jean think?

The nagging voice in my head spoke to me again, "*Coward*".

My jaw clenched with anxious energy, my throat tensed and I felt my voice wavering as a said, "I'm not quitting."

My friend on the other end let out a long sigh, "All I needed to know. When you get back, I'll still be here man. You owe me a song." he said and hung up the phone.

I placed the phone back in my jacket pocket and looked at the papers laying next to me. Smirking, I glanced at Pennon.

"Yah, yah, no more need for those instructions. I'll set course right away." the lizard said and pushed himself to his feet. He turned around and sauntered to the driver's panel.

I saw Bosun give me an inquisitive look, I said "I assume you overheard?"

He nodded his head, but his hands still firmly gripped the pistol. "You only have to worry about him for now," I said and pointed at the mercenary.

"Okay," Bosun said and relaxed his shoulders, letting them droop down into a more comfortable position. He still held the pistol, but he let his arms fall to his sides.

I felt a sudden lurch of the ship. Looking at Pennon, I could see a small smirk on his face. He flipped a final switch, the ship burst forward, racing towards the planet's atmosphere. The G-forces were pulling me towards the back of the ship, I grabbed the closest cabinet handle and held on.

I closed my eyes and tried to focus on breathing, but my motion sick stomach refused to calm. I could hear the rushing wind outside the ship, the air angry that it was being displaced. The insides of my ears felt like they would burst with pressure as we reached new heights. I swallowed and my ears popped, relieving the pressure.

Suddenly the ship jolted, sending a shock wave through my bones. Then another thrust and another, we were breaking through each level of atmosphere. With each barrier we surpassed my knees ached a little more, physics itself attempting to knock me down.

Then, with no warning, after one final push forward, the weight of the world left my shoulders. My feet left the ground, I pointed my toes down to tap the floor and with that simple force my body floated higher. I opened my eyes and looked towards the front windshield, it was the same starry night I had noticed before. I pirouetted around to look out the back window, Terradin, my home, was the size of a classroom globe from up here.

...

It had been several hours since we set our course, the ship was in autopilot now. Everyone aboard the ship were trying to entertain themselves. Pennon sitting next to the mini fridge sipping a beer. Bosun had holstered the pistol and opted to continue leaning against the wall. The canine was absentmindedly playing with the Merc's credit stick, bending it with a hand on each end of the stick for a few moments and then releasing the pressure for another couple of seconds.

The mercenary still sat in the center of the ship, crossed legged and keeping his head down. Maybe he hoped his captors were like the mighty T-rex, if he didn't move maybe we couldn't see him. I had checked his phone further and searched on my laptop for whatever I could find about those coordinates with no luck. Whatever operation was going on down there, the sons kept it quiet.

Sitting on the bench, I leaned forward and rested my elbows on my knees. "What's your name?" I asked the young mercenary.

The man's body jumped in recognition that he was being questioned. Keeping his head down he mumbled in response.

My lizard companion glared at the mumbler, "Speak up, the old man can't hear you," he said.

I raised one of my eyebrows at the Hylathan, "Stop calling me old man, I'm Martin." I said.

The thief chuckled, "Alright, Marty."

Rolling my eyes, I focused again on our captive, "Your name?" I asked again.

The mercenary lifted his head slightly, and peered at me. "Jackson," he said.

I locked my eyes on his, "Jackson, what is happening on Altay?" I asked.

The young man's eyes did not look away from mine, "I don't know. We were only transporting people there." he said, his voice was steady.

Bosun's ears perked up, "Don't think he's lying," he said.

"And how would you know that, Dog?" Pennon said, about to sip from his drink.

Bosun put pressure on the credit stick in his hands again. "I could hear it in his voice," he said.

"Course you could," the Hylathan said sarcastically. "That begs the question, why didn't you 'hear' it earlier when you had him by the throat?"

My canine companion looked away guiltily, "Didn't want ta hear it. Too angr-" a loud snap was heard and his sentence cut short. He had broke Jackson's credit stick in half, and now stared bewildered for a moment at his blunder. Then his face turned sad.

I could see tears line the rims of his eyes, as he continued to stare down at the broken device, his ears drooping forward and his forehead lined with wrinkles. "Sorry," he placed the pieces down gently beside him, "Wanna find em', is all," he sniffled.

I glanced at Pennon, he had frozen in his nonchalant drinking pose, but his eyes crinkled around the edges slightly with what appeared to be guilt.

The lizard sighed and set down his can beside him, "If it was my girl missing, I'd be in the same state." he said. His fiery eyes flickered from Bosun to the can of alcohol, picking it back up and shrugging he said coolly, "Don't beat yourself up about it."

The dog's ears shot up and his large jowls curled into a smile, his eyes were still sad, but his tail wagged behind him. Pennon looked bashfully away and took a large swig.

I smiled at the Newfoundland, then smirked at the lizard. Such different characters these two, but I'm beginning to think deep down they both are good people. I glanced at the young man in my captivity, maybe there's a chance he's good deep down too.

I slowly stood up, the low gravity made moving easier on my old joints. Walking, more like skipping with how every step brought me up to then float down, over to the mini fridge I grabbed a cold one. Then I sauntered to the young Jackson, bent down and held the can in front of him.

"Here," I said.

The mercenary stared at me pensively, then slowly reached out and took the beer from my hand. He watched intently as I returned to the red bench to sit down, cautiously he brought his other hand to the tab. What followed was the loud pop and hiss of the condensed air of the carbonated beverage being released. After a few more seconds, he took a hesitant sip.

"Jackson, I know you're frightened. You have every reason to be." I said.

The man nodded solemnly, then brought the beer to his lips again and took a gulp.

"No matter what you do, you're in a rough spot," I said, leaning back and folding my arms across my chest. "But if you make our lives easier, we'll return the favor."

Pennon's stare burned into the side of my head, "We are *not* letting him go." he said. He clenched the can in his hand, his claws cut into the aluminum without resistance and liquid dripped from his fingers.

I put my hand up in a calming gesture, "We aren't going to let you go, but you'll be left to the Manzala justice system after all this if you help us."

I said. "You have to admit that, with the pickle you're in, that is the best outcome for you." I shrugged.

A dismayed look was plastered over Jackson's face, "And what would I do?" he said.

"Well, I'm sure your comrades would be happy to let you in when they find out you secured the Hylathan and his friends." I said.

The young man's eyes widened, "I can't do that! They'll kill me." he croaked.

"Only if they find out." Pennon stated flatly.

Bosun leaned forward, "If yah help, I won't let em' touch yah," he said, genuine determination across his features.

Jackson stared at the muscular dog in shock, his mouth agape. Pennon began laughing so hard, he bent over holding his shaking chest with his free hand.

"Sorry, but," the lizard chuckled, then took a moment to gasp for breath, "You might not be the best person to offer that."

The dog's ears flattened back, his tail swayed slowly. He looked away bashfully, "I mean it though," he said.

The mercenary raised an eyebrow, "You're all legitimately insane...and I have no choice in this, do I?" his voice shook.

I let out a small laugh, "No, not really Jack." I said.

...

Thick, orange, gas clouds passed the window as the ship flew into planet Altay's atmosphere.

Pennon standing at the controls, gripping the throttle and with the other hand pressing button after button. The hull shook and rattled, as the reddish brown planets ground rushed up to meet us.

As we came closer the many dark veins of canyons running across Altay grew more immense. The hylathan captain widened his stance, "Don't panic." he said.

Bosun scowled, "Why'd we panic?" he said.

With a smirk, the lizard grabbed onto the ships yoke and with both hands pressed it down. The aircrafts nose suddenly pointed down and my stomach leapt into my throat. I clenched my hands down on the bench I was sitting on, the speed at which we were approaching the surface was increasing.

Bosun held onto one of the cabinet handles, his ears and jowls pulled back from the g-force. Jackson sitting on the floor, started to slide towards the back of the ship. He dropped his beer and let the can roll away as he grasped at the floor. I turned my head back to the front of the ship. My eyes were locked onto the windshield, watching the geography below become more detailed.

"Pull up, pull up!" the young man screamed.

With another push on the yoke, Pennon sent us downward even faster. Jackson screamed again, as we were only seconds away from colliding with the surface of Altay.

With a jerking turn to the left, we entered into a canyon, the further down we fell the more the unbreathable gases faded. The ship's spotlights lit up the increasing darkness of the canyon. Finally our scaly captain pulled up and we were level with the canyon floor.

For a few minutes the ship soared between the massive rock walls, in the distance lights appeared and grew brighter. The techo-dwarven starport, a glowing beacon for us weary travelers. I observed the massive grey concrete pillars lining the front of the building, bright green lights lining them on all sides.

The building itself looked bunker-like, it had a sloping concrete roof. Its top half was lined with windows, probably filled with security forces watching our approach. The lower half was filled with ship hangar openings spaced between the pillars.

Slowing down, we flew towards the front-most hangar, and entered in. Gently the ship touched down, and the ramp began to open. Jackson scrambled to his feet and pressed himself against the wall, I stood up from the bench. Bosun walked over to the lowering ramp and stood waiting in front of it.

Finally, the ramp made contact with the hangar floor and the four of us walked out. At the bottom of the ship's walkway three armed techno-dwarvesin uniform watched us. They all wore matching green and grey ensembles; each individual only had slight variations in the patches adorning their garbs and various accessories.

They were filed side by side in front of the ramp. The leftmost dwarf, the only one wearing an officer's beret, hailed us in a booming voice, "Dr. Glenmont's troop?" A rifle was gripped in his hands.

I nodded, "Are you his, ah, 'confidants?'" I asked.

"Yes. You are Mr. Aten?" he answered.

I nodded again and pointed towards my crew, "The Xenoform is Bosun, the other human is Jackson, and the Hylathan is Pennon. He may need a little medical assistance before we go anywhere." I said.

The officer nodded and looked us up, then down, with his steely green eyes. In some ways, he looked similar to Glenmont. Out of the three, he was the most physically imposing, standing several inches taller than the others, and his posture was the strictest. He turned his head to look at Jackson. When I saw the left side of his face I held back a gasp. Several branching scars fanned out around his mandible, and a jagged chunk was missing from his ear.

"My name is Pierce," he said and holstered his rifle on his back.

The rightmost dwarf puffed up, "Stein," he said introducing himself.

Stein, unlike his clean-shaven compatriots, had a slight stubble. His uniform, upon closer inspection, wasn't iron-pressed like the others either, it was wrinkled. He wore green goggles that wrapped snugly around his head. He'd clearly tried to comb down his red hair, but the sides stuck out in frizzy bits.

The dwarf next to the unkempt red-head spoke up, "Marsha."

Marsha had her sleek, black hair cut into a short bob and her uniform was impeccable. Her face was young and a little round, but her blue eyes were just as sharp as the officer's. She was wearing a tool belt with many pockets and a bandoleer lined with small canisters. She had a pistol in a hip holster and a tactical shotgun in her hands.

I stepped further down the ramp and looked around the hangar. This huge, brightly lit, open space was filled with bustling dwarven security and engineers. Many parked ships being loaded with cargo, the large metal containers most likely filled with resources mined here on Altay.

The steely officer glanced at me, then directed his gaze at Jackson. "The sons have no business being here," he turned around on his heel and began walking away, "We'll blow the bastards out of the fucking water," he said, his voice had a scalpel sharp tone to it.

Marsha began walking away as well and Stein motioned us to follow.

SIX

My CALLOUSED fingers strummed the coiled steel strings of my acoustic guitar. I hummed the melody as Sylvester quietly sung along. We were relaxing on my cool back porch. My Jean listened from the open kitchen window as she prepared lunch. My eyes were closed, but the pleasantly warm sunlight shone through my eyelids and covered my perception with a comfortable orange hue.

A light breeze blew by and I swayed my head to my guitar's rhythm, the song so practiced I could play it while asleep. The mahogany fingerboard met the tips of my fingers, the bright tone of the strings' reverberations carrying the three of us along. I opened my eyes and they adjusted to the light.

Sylvester's curly hair bobbed as he nodded along with the beat, his signature smile plain across his face as he sang. The corners of his eyes crinkled with joy when the chorus returned; I couldn't help but chuckle. We made an odd pair of friends, living very different lives. What started as a business acquaintanceship turned into a friendship based on a love for music. Warily trading information for credits in poorly lit clubs became song-filled sunny Saturdays in my backyard.

I could hear Jean clapping along with the song, Sylvester looked at her and laughed, he began to clap along too. I looked up, letting more of the sun's warmth caress my skin. The sky shone a perfect blue, the large tree on my property swayed and rustled in the wind. A hundred green leaves on each branch reached out in every direction, moving my eyes to its trunk I saw at the base my old boy. My black and white Boston Terrier, napping in the tree's shade. In dog years he was probably older than me now; Maxwell yawned and rolled onto his back in the thick grass.

The back screen-door to the house creaked as Jean carried a tray of scones. She stepped gracefully onto the patio and placed the tray onto the ornate metal outdoor table in front of me. I stopped playing the guitar and Sylvester scooted his chair closer to the table. Jean sat down in the chair next to me, and after putting down my guitar into a stand on my left I turned to her.

She's just as old as me, but her looks have not diminished over the years. Short brown hair peppered with grey, styled into a pixie cut. Dark brown eyes that shine with attentiveness and care, small crow's feet at the corners of her eyes the only sign of age in them. Thin lips shaped into a cupid's bow smile, that smile was turned towards me.

She'd dressed in casual blue jeans and a purple sleeveless blouse, her slender freckled arms resting on the table. Her slim, smooth hands retrieved a waiting mystery novel. We'd married young and now we enjoyed the fruits of decades of labor, enjoying song, scones, and sun.

"Didn't you finish that book last week?" Sylvester asked Jean.

My wife's eyebrows furrowed a little, "I just started reading this one."

I reached for a scone and brought it to my mouth, chewing slowly I focused on the buttery sweet flavor. Swallowing, I glanced over the cover of the novel and laughed.

"Syl's right. You said the twist was that the detective was dead all along." I said.

Jean gasped, "Don't spoil the story!" as Syl and I chuckled, she jokingly punched my shoulder.

...

A firm hand shook my shoulder, I started awake; sunny dreams fading into harsh florescent lighting. I blinked a couple of times, clearing the sleep from my eyes, then looked up to see Stein sitting next to me.

"Wake up," he said, tinkering with what looked like a metal backpack. "We're getting close."

A low rumble underpinned all sound, and after a few moments I remembered where I was: Packed into a High Mobility Military Grav Vehicle, with Officer Pierce at the steering wheel. We hastily hovered across the stony canyon floor, heading for the coordinates.

The vehicle had traditional driver and front-passenger seats, but the back seats were set against the walls, allowing more space to set up equipment in the middle. Stein was on my left, Jackson was on my right. I glanced at the young man. He gave me a worried look; it was understandable that he would be stressed, given that he was going to betray his employers for us. Marsha, sitting across from the mercenary, leaned forward, snapping a tracker strap around Jackson's right wrist.

Jackson flinched, "That's too tight," he said.

"Good, means there's no getting away," Marsha said.

To the left of Marsha sat Bosun, scrunching his shoulders and knees together to properly fit in his seat. Next sat Pennon, sprawled slightly into Bosun's seat, his eyes half-lidded. His whole body appeared relaxed; I guessed he'd gotten dosed with some form of painkiller. I was glad to see he was properly bandaged, though I was a little worried about his drugged state.

"You're not too tired, are you?" I asked the drowsy looking lizard.

Pennon lazily flitted his eyes towards me, "I'm just enjoyin' this down swing. When we arrive I'll hit a stim." he mumbled.

I looked through the rear window, there wasn't much of a view. I thought back to the briefing Pierce had with us at the starport, the facility we were traveling to was registered as a techno-dwarf ore testing site. When Pierce's scouts looked into it, they reported that something wasn't right. The traffic flowing in and out of the building was not consistent with normal patterns for other sites, and though the majority of workers there should be techno-dwarves, only a small number could be observed among the other employees.

I looked at Pierce, "You said we had a way to locate the engine once inside?"

Stein looked up from the bulky device on his

lap, "I'm so in tune with tech, I'll sniff out that engine," he jabbed his thumb towards himself, his gnarled teeth exposed in a grin.

I raised an eyebrow in suspicion, but the techno-dwarf simply smirked back at me. "For instance, you have a phone, laptop and a Flat-"

"Okay, okay. I get it, I get it." I interrupted him, heat rushing to my cheeks.

Both Bosun and Pennon's heads snapped up to stare at me, surprised by my reaction. They both wore nonplussed expressions.

The redheaded Stein waved his hands to put the focus back onto him, "Dog, you have a broken credit stick yes?" he pointed at the canine. "Hand it over," Steins eyes shone brightly from behind his green lens goggles.

My furry friend furrowed his brow, but took the broken pieces of the credit stick from his pocket and offered it up into the redhead's open palm.

Stein threw out his hand and poked a single finger on one of the broken bits. In a sudden flash of light, the item was whole again.

Bosun's ears and eyebrows shot up in shock, his eyes frantically flicked from his hand to the smirking redhead.

"Abracadabra!" Stein laughed, waving his outstretched hand in a flourish.

"Magic," the canine breathlessly mouthed.

Marsha pushed a piece of her hair behind her ear, "We were trained to be militarily competent, but also trained in the Arcane to have an edge over our enemies," she said.

Stein slowly clasped his hands together, "The perfect blend of tech and as you said 'magic'."

"Exciting," Pennon said, "So can all of you--?" he sleepily yawned.

"In different ways," Marsha said, her piercing blue eyes intently observing our reactions.

The large dog's mouth still hung agape; through his eyes one could almost see the inner gears of his mind grinding frantically in an attempt to understand this revelation.

"No idea what that means," Bosun said.

Marsha's eyes crinkled. She stifled a giggle, and instantly returned to her serious expression.

"We're on point," Pierce announced.

The vehicle slowed to a stop and we filed out into the open air. Stein picked up a large metal crate from the top of the rig and set it down on the ground. Taking the lid off, he pointed to the contents.

"There's a pistol, two loaded mags and a body camera in each individual pouch," Stein said.

Marsha leaned over and began handing out the pouches to each of us, finally coming to Jackson. She strapped the body camera to his chest, then took the pistol, emptied the mags of bullets, then handed him back the now-impotent weapon.

Jackson pressed his lips firmly together in a displeased fashion as he placed the weapon in his holster. We all put on the cameras and holstered our pistols. I watched as Marsha prepared her shotgun, loaded the shells, and pumped the hand grip. Finally, she put on the canister bandoleer over her chest.

Stein put the crate back atop the vehicle and picked up the metal backpack he had been working on earlier. He tapped his fingers across the top of it and the backpack began to shake. Jackson took a scared step backwards. Marsha tightly grabbed his wrist to keep him in place.

Suddenly, the device before our eyes began to grow. Arms and legs sprouted forth from the thing and finally a head, the smooth metallic creature stood two feet taller than Stein. Even though its stature was only slightly larger than the average dwarf, its bright copper-like eyes intimidated me.

Pennon, still too drugged to be surprised, pulled out the syringe full of stimulant the medics back at the starport had given him. He jammed the needle in his arm and his whole body shivered as though hit with a chilled wind. He shook his head, then fully opened his amber eyes. His pupils began huge, but quickly narrowed down to slim slits.

"This another magic trick?" the lizard asked.

Stein grinned, "You could call it that. Say hello to Franky,"

The construct slowly waved hello. Bosun waved back and stared with intense curiosity. The redhead reached into his tool belt and whipped out an ornate metal cube the size of a large apple.

"This is what we are looking for, a Dwarven Engine," Stein held out the cube for all of us to see. "Of course, Glenmont's will be slightly different, but in general this is what they look like." Bosun and I made sure to get a good look; Pennon appeared uninterested.

"I've seen it," said the hylathan, his breath continuing to accelerate as the stim took hold.

Pierce stepped over, holding a tablet, "Your body cams are all connected to this," he pointed to the device in his hand. "Just around the corner of this canyon is the back entrance of the ore research facility,"

Pierce pointed to Jackson, "You are going to convince the guards at the door that you captured the hylathan," he gestured to Pennon.

Jackson's eyes were wide, "There's no way this will work," he said, nervously glancing at my scaled companion. The young man dropped his head and stared at his feet. All things considered, this was risky, and as much I trusted Glenmont's compatriots I felt uneasy. The mercs' original plan involved sending Pennon's chopped bits here; I didn't place much stock in the facility's billing as a simple ore mine.

"Once inside, Stein can point out the general direction of the Engine," Pierce said.

Bosun's tail shot up, "What about Gordon?"

The leader gave the canine an understanding look, "Unfortunately, we don't have a sure-fire way to track him. However, once we locate the engine with any luck your brother won't be far."

I patted the furry one's shoulder, "You'll sniff him out," I said.

Bosun's face was still worn with worry, but his tail wagged a little in appreciation of my consolation.

I turned to Pennon, he was stretching his shoulders and fidgeting his feet. After that Stimulant, he must be really rearing to go.

The lizard stared at Jackson with a hungry look in his fiery eyes, "Finally gonna smash some sons heads," he stated, punching the air. "Ever see one of us shed our skin, Merc?"

Jackson shook his head, his face went a few shades paler.

The Hylathan smirked, his sharp teeth poking out in threatening points, "You will."

"Head out, we'll be watching from here," the leader held up his tablet.

Marsha nodded and shotgun in hand she motioned the anxious mercenary to follow her. The lizard clasped his hands behind his back and followed behind them, pretending to be their prisoner.

Pierce leaned the tablet against a rock for all of us to watch. While the screen flickered, the leader sat down and pulled out all his loaded magazines. Placing them flat on the ground in front of him, he began waving his hands over the mags and muttering. A light aura like glow appeared around the magazines as he did this.

Bosun's ears shot up, "More magic?"

Pierce did not turn, but Stein looked up to Bosun and simply gave him a little grin and a nod.

"Magic bullets," the canine said in awe.

My focus turned to the tablet; three view points were clear. They were approaching a daunting brown concrete structure crammed into the canyon. The back entrance was a large doorway with two armed, intimidating guards wearing the same black uniform as Jackson.

"Remember—you screw this up. I shoot you first," Marsha whispered to the young mercenary.

I could hear the young man gulp with fear.

As they approached, the guards noticed them and pointed their rifles. "Identify yourselves!" the guard on the right yelled.

"I-Identification number is 26823," Jackson said, his voice cracking a little.

They continued walking forward, I could clearly see the expressions on the guards' faces now.

"What about her and the snake?" the guard on the right grunted.

Marsha stepped forward, "The hylathan is our prisoner, and I work with your employer." She put out her left hand and waved in greeting.

Something changed all of a sudden in the guard's expressions. Their faces relaxed and their eyelids drooped down slightly, as though they became incredibly bored with the conversation. The guard on the left took out a small electronic tablet and started pressing buttons lazily.

The guard looked back up from the tablet and squinted at Jackson. "Yep, you're who you say you are. It's reported here you were missing in action after pursuing one target and two others." he looked back down at the tablet and frowned slightly, "How'd you get here? Why didn't you report in sooner?"

Jackson started to stammer when Marsha took another step closer, "We came here in my personal craft," she threw out her left hand in a strange flourish. "Knowing how much our employer wanted the hylathan, we thought it would make a nice surprise."

The guards slowly nodded, and she waved her hand again. "26823 here did such an amazing job incapacitating the two others and capturing the target, he deserves a hero's welcome. Least of all a chance to impress our Balil Prince."

The guard's continued nodding with vacant

expressions, the guard on the right said in a monotone voice, "That is impressive. Alright, we'll let you in."

The guard on the left paused for a short moment absentmindedly staring at the tablet in his hand. His eyebrows knitted together in confusion, then he stared up at Marsha.

"Wait." he said, "Who are you exactly?"

I could hear Jackson start to hyperventilate and Pennon hiss under his breath.

Marsha took another few steps, she was so close that I could see the Guard's pupils. She waved her hand again, wiggling her fingers as they went past her body-cam. "I already told you and you verified it." She pointed at the tablet.

"Please tell me, they didn't put memory deficient men to guard here. Did they?" she asked in an annoyed tone.

Both the guards pupils grew as big as olives, and their faces eased even further. The guard on the right elbowed the other in the side.

The guard on the left flinched then scratched his head, "S-sorry, you're right. It won't happen again... Ma'am," he said.

They opened the door and led my companions inside. The camera feed flashed brightly as the body-cams adjusted to the light inside the building. Everyone had shuffled into a boring, beige hallway; Marsha rotated around and I spotted the security camera over the door from her feed. My heart began to pound.

The techno-dwarf reached to her bandoleer and clicked a button on the top canister. I heard a muffled whirring coming from her device. She faced the guards and peered behind them, the hallway ended in a closed door. "Do we go that way?" She pointed at the door.

The guard closest to her shook his head, "That's just a restroom," he pointed towards the other end of the hallway. "You'll go that way."

Marsha spun on her heel and looked where the guard had pointed. The hallway was a few paces long and turned to the left. The whirring noise stopped and she slowly turned to face the guards again.

Subtly, she removed the metal canister from her bandoleer, and let it clatter to the floor. The guards blinked, their tired expressions being replaced with confusion. Suddenly, the canister split in half and a black sphere popped up. With a flash it displayed a large mirror image of all of them simply standing in the hallway and talking.

I gasped with surprise, that's how she'll get past the camera. The canister is a MirrorSphere, originally designed to keep maintenance workers out of sight. It scans an environment and displays an image around it. People outside the MirrorSphere's 'bubble' only see the previous scan, whilst whatever is inside is isolated from view.

The two guards visages turned to distress. Suddenly Marsha grabbed the hand of the closest guard and began muttering. The guard's eyes went wide with shock, his pupils rolled back, his whole body went limp and then he crashed to the floor. His rifle skittering across the ground.

My eyes flitted to Pennon's camera feed, the lizard had already unclasped his hands from behind his back and was swinging a fist at the other guard's head. The guard, concerned with his fallen friend, didn't even see the incoming blow.

Pennon's knuckles cracked across back of the man's skull and the guard slumped to the floor, out cold.

"Alright, move in," Marsha said. "The ruse won't last forever."

I looked away from the tablet and turned to Pierce. He holstered his rifle and pistol, picked up the tablet, and slipped the device into his coat. Then he nodded to Stein. The redheaded techno-dwarf and his construct ran towards the facility, followed closely by Pierce stomping towards the building. Bosun and I followed him around the corner. We quickly entered the building, passing through the MirrorSphere's bubble. Pennon was standing over the guard he knocked out, removing the unconscious man's uniform.

Marsha was directing Jackson to drag the guard she sent to sleep into the nearby restroom. Stein stood on his construct's shoulders next to the doorway. The machine's legs extended to allow Stein to reach the security camera over the entrance. He was carefully opening the camera with the tools from his belt.

Gaining access to the wiring, the Construct-Creator put his tools away at his waist. He reached down, "Franky, give me an eye, will you?"

The construct brought one of its hands to its left eye; with a few clicks it removed a chunk of his face. The machine's eye still flitted about in its socket as it reached the entire chunk up to Stein's waiting palm.

"All right, buddy. We're gonna hook you up to

the mainline." the redhead stared at the blinking eye though his goggles. "I'm counting on you, don't let anybody know we're here," he said.

Stein quickly unplugged a wire and just as fast connected Franky's eye. He jumped down from the construct's shoulders and asked, "You in?"

The construct's remaining eye blinked frantically for a moment, then became calm. The machine gave its creator a thumbs-up; in response, Stein's smile brimmed with pride.

The MirrorSphere turned off and the illusion dropped.

Bosun stepped beside me and frowned, "They... can't see us?" He pointed at the modified security camera.

The Construct-Creator beamed proudly, "Franky is altering the feed in real time, repeating the MirrorSphere's original loop. We're invisible to anyone viewing the stream at the moment."

The canine nodded his head and held his chin, "Magic," he whispered.

Stein laughed, "No, technology."

The furry mutt frowned, then shrugged.

I turned around to look at the others, Jackson had finished placing the guard in the bathroom and stooped down to begin dragging the guard now lacking a uniform. Marsha stared at the young mercenary as he struggled to pull the unconscious man.

Bosun walked over and lifted the legs of the man, helping Jackson to lift him up. Pennon wearing the uniform, slipped into the ill-fitting black jacket. The lizard then walked over to stand beside the young merc.

The hylathan leaned in towards Jackson, "Have you seen one of us shed our skin?"

Jackson was now holding the man up, his arms were shaking and his breathing was heavy. He sighed, annoyed, "I already told yo-" his sentence cut short as he looked up at Pennon.

The lizard's scales began to crawl along his body, like a thousand blue beetles. His muzzle, tail, and razor sharp claws seemed to melt away, leaving clammy pink skin in their wake. The scales sunk into the pastel flesh, and splotches of blonde hair protruded from his head.

After those few mind-boggling moments, the reptilian was replaced with a perfect copy of the unconscious guard in Jackson's hands. The mercenary gasped in fear and lurched forward, nearly dropping the guard on his head. His young troubled eyes were huge with fear and disgust.

The shapeshifted Pennon smirked and turned to Marsha. "So, that magic shit," he held up his hands and wriggled his new porcelain smooth fingers. "We going to hypnotize our way through here?"

Marsha shrugged, and picked up the MirrorSphere canister. "It's suggestion, and hopefully we won't have to. There's a cost to everything, and convincing someone against their best interests is difficult, even with the arcane."

The shape-shifted lizard nodded thoughtfully, and Marsha put the used canister in a back pocket.

Once the unconscious guards were stored in the restroom, Pierce motioned all of us to follow him down the hallway. Pierce took the lead, Marsha was second in line, then me, Pennon, Bosun, Jackson,

Stein, and Franky the construct. We strode along the corridor, the muffled sounds of our steps softly tapping across the solid concrete floor.

We approached the left turn at the end of the hallway. Pierce pressed himself against the wall and peered around the corner, after a few moments he waved his hand and Marsha led us forward. The leader stayed at the corner keeping watch. I followed the others.

Doors lined the short corridor's walls, filling me with unease. This hallway continued forward for a long ways. A few paces away, another corridor connected to the left. Marsha looked back and glanced at Stein, his eyes oddly strained. The redhead nodded at her.

Marsha looked forward again, took a few steps forward, and froze. Suddenly, muffled speaking could be heard approaching from the closest door to the right. The sounds grew louder from behind the closed door and my heart felt like it was going to burst from my chest.

Pierce quickly shuffled passed to the front of us and placed his hand on his second-in-command's shoulder. She nodded and threw out her hands in front of her, staring intently forward. The door began to rattle and the muffled speaking sounds became louder.

Pierce waved for us to run around the left corner ahead. Everyone jogged past Marsha and hid around the corner while she stood there, holding the door closed with her arcane skills. Whoever was behind the door began to shake the handle and yell.

Once all of us pressed ourselves against the left corridor's walls, Marsha sprinted over to join us.

She let down her hands and held her head, grimacing. Using her abilities so much in such a short time frame had clearly taken a toll. We heard the door open and several loud voices exclaiming angrily as they passed through.

We firmly pressed ourselves against the wall, hoping that we wouldn't be seen. I held my breath as the voices approached and became clearer.

"We'll need to inform maintenance about that door, with the Prince here we can't have that happen to him," said one gruff voice.

"Heard he's apparently in a good mood with the project ready for testing," spoke a monotone male voice.

I saw the two guards sauntering in front of us. One turn. Just one turn of their heads and they would see us. I clenched my hand over the handle of my holstered pistol, ready for what seemed inevitable.

The gruff voice coughed and began speaking again, "Good. Means we might finally end this godforsaken job."

"I hope so. After seeing everything here, I might just retire and use my cash to start a normal business. Maybe sell rugs, or furniture. Open a restaurant. Something, anyways," said the monotone voice.

They walked past our hallway and out of sight, I held back a sigh of relief.

Their voices got quieter as they got farther away, "I don't blame you, thought I'd seen it all. The sons are on a completely different level," the gruff voice laughed. "Rugs?" he asked.

The speaking became barely audible, and a few moments later the hallway became silent.

We all glanced at one, another waiting for a cue to make our next move. Pierce's steely eyes turned to Stein.

"Engine?" the leader asked.

Stein flitted his eyes from one direction to another, then pointed down the hallway following the guards. Pierce took a moment, a calculating look on his face. He turned down the hallway we were hiding in and looked around.

"What kind of tech is in this room?" Pierce asked and pointed towards a door across the hallway from us.

Stein repeated his searching glare, "Headsets...tablets," his eyebrows shot up. "Laser Rifles, lots of them," he said.

Marsha put her hands back down from her head, "Their equipment room?"

Pennon chuckled, "Or a break room filled with armed guards." The disguised hylathan cracked his knuckles and smirked, "I'll take care of this."

Bosun's ears shot up and he gave the lizard a worried look, "Yer sure about that?"

"You're not getting too attached to me are you, mutt?" The guard-impostor mocked.

Jackson standing next to the large canine, his eyes nervously flicking from side to side stepped forward. "He's right, I'll go with you for safety," he said.

Pennon squinted his fiery eyes, "Bullshit." He moved his fierce stare to the dog, "If you want to help, keep an eye on that snake," he pointed at the young captive.

Bosun looked between Pennon and Jackson. "Wait," he said. "I thought you were..."

Pennon simply shook his head, scoffing a bit at Bosun, then looked to Pierce.

Pierce nodded, "We'll watch through your body-cam, get in there."

The human-appearing reptilian nodded and stood in front of the door. Our leader took out the tablet and opened Pennon's stream. The hylathan put his hand on the doorknob, turned the handle, and slipped inside the room.

Once he was out of sight, I immediately turned my eyes towards the tablet. I observed the room and noticed the walls were covered in metal shelving, lined with boxes. I sighed with relief—*not* a cafeteria.

"Weren't you stationed at the back?" a bored voice asked Pennon.

The lizard impostor turned towards the speaker, I gulped with anxiety. Three uniformed guards were sorting boxes at the back of the room, the most hulking of them was a green skinned Orc.

"I am, but my headset started squelching in my ear for no reason. Which one of these boxes have the extras?" the shape-shifter coolly said.

The orc nodded, and pointed to one of the shelves. The guards went back to work and Pennon strode over to the boxes. The body-cam caught more of his surroundings, on the opposite wall from where the lizard entered was a door. On the far wall across from the guards, to the left of the entrance Pennon came from, was a third door.

The hylathan reached into one of the boxes,

rummaging around and stalling as he and the rest of us tried to decide our next move.

"Did you hear what shit they slapped onto the project," one of the guards, a stout xenoform rooster said.

The orc huffed, "I don't need any more nightmares, bud."

The rooster chuckled, "What are you..." the orc rolled his eyes, "Chicken?" the rooster said.

A third guard, a cybernetic enhanced human spoke up, "hylathan wings, right?" His entire jaw was replaced with chrome implants.

"Disgusting," the orc sighed.

Pennon froze for a moment and nonchalantly turned towards the guards, "I'm supposed to guard the project next shift," he said.

"That sucks," the rooster said.

"Hey this is going to sound moronic, but...how do I get to that room?" the reptilian impostor said, feigning embarrassment.

The orc raised an eyebrow, "Seriously?" he pointed to the door opposite where Pennon had entered. "From here you go through that door, turn left, go right, and then the lab is to the right," he said.

The rooster chortled, "You gotta stop drinking, man."

Before Pennon could respond, we heard the sound of the door on the back wall open.

From behind the hylathan, a baritone voice said, "Hey boys? Something's off, the guys in the back have just been standin' around talking to some chick." Pennon whipped around to face the speaker.

"I keep radioing them, but-" The speaker cut off his sentence when he saw Pennon's disguised face.

The short, human guard stood stock still, the door he came through was still open and in the room beyond multiple security streams played across a large screen. I squinted my eyes and made out the camera feed from the back entrance, still streaming a loop of the two guards we had knocked out talking to Marsha, Jackson, and Pennon.

Our reptilian impostor held up the new headset, "Sorry about that, headset was haywire. Just got here to replace it."

The short man's expression was pure confusion, the rooster spoke, "What's this about a chick?"

The confused guard said, "He was talking to a girl and one of us, they have a hylathan..." His eyes flitted to Pennon, staring for a moment as his eyebrows began to rise.

Slowly he turned to look back at the security screen, now even slower. Pallid and clammy, he turned back to face the disguised lizard. His eyes were wide with terror, his mouth quivered and his voice squeaked as he tried to form words.

Pierce turned off the tablet and put it away. Quickly, he picked a pistol magazine, loaded it into the pistol, and cocked the gun. Holstering the pistol, then he picked another magazine, he loaded it into his rifle, chambered the first round, and holstered the rifle.

Stein and Marsha both readied their weapons and took point on both sides of the door. Franky stood behind the redhead on the left side of the door. Marsha held her shotgun tightly in one hand and grabbed the door handle with the other.

Finally catching on, I readied my pistol. I looked at Bosun, his ears were straight up and his hands were shaking. I glanced at the nervous Jackson beside the canine. I nodded at the dog to get his attention, my furry friend's eyes locked onto mine. I motioned to my gun, trying to communicate for him to ready his firearm.

That's when Marsha turned the handle and Pierce stormed through with his pistol, I whipped my head towards the action. The short, clever guard was raising his handgun. But Pierce was lightning-fast, and his glowing gun fired in the moment between when the guard's cleverness revealed him as a threat and the moment when the guard's reflexes would have sent a bullet at Pennon.

The blast stunned me with its immensity, a shock wave of sound rolling in a radius around Pierce. The wall behind the short guard blossomed in an almost-symetrical pattern of blood-red stain. The man's face tensed, and he grabbed his chest for only a moment before crumpling to the ground.

I opened my eyes, the right lens of my glasses had a small crack in the corner. I glanced back to my canine friend and my stomach leapt into my throat, behind the cringing Newfoundland, Jackson was sprinting down the hallway, seizing the chaos to flee us to his fellows.

"Bosun!" I yelled, my voice sounded muted due to the ringing in my ears.

The dog looked to me and followed my line of sight. His shaking hands un-holstered his pistol and he pointed the barrel at Jackson's fleeing back. I didn't want Jackson dead; the young man had simply made a poor decision in becoming a mercenary. But if he got away—what would happen to us?

Bosun's gun shook violently in his hands. Jackson neared the end of the hallway, close to turning out of our sight. The canine tensed, he steadied his hands. I held my breath and awaited the shot.

Jackson glanced back at us. His face filled with fear, not unlike the expression he held on Pennon's ship, while furry hands wrapped around his throat. The muscular canine's tail curled down between his legs and he lowered the pistol with a sigh. The young man rushed around the left corner and was gone.

I heard a loud slamming, two laser shots, and a shotgun blast from behind me. Bosun and I ran to the doorway. The three guards in back had pulled down one of the metal shelves to use as cover. They crouched behind the overturned shelf, holding some of the laser rifles that had clattered to the floor.

Franky's right shoulder smoked from a laser shot, he was standing in front of his creator, shielding him. Pennon had dropped his disguise and crouched on the ground. Marsha strafed over to the hylathan, shotgun pointed at the guards

Pierce holstered his pistol and readied his rifle, an orange aura glowed around the weapon. An alarm began to sound across the facility, a steady, high-pitched wail that made my already damaged hearing throb with pain.

Only a few seconds had passed when the three

guards burst up to fire upon us. The cybernetically-enhanced man was missing his metal jaw, presumably from the earlier fire. His chin was replaced with a jagged hole, filled with broken teeth and a tongue hanging down.

I fought back the urge to throw up, as Pierce fired his arcane bullet. With one shot the bullet split into multiple projectiles, slamming into the guard's bodies. They didn't even get the chance to fire back, their blood painting the walls and some droplets splattering on the ceiling. The alarms were still blaring in my ears, the smell of fresh blood hit my nostrils and I retched.

"We need to get moving now!" Marsha yelled.

Pennon got back up to his feet, "Where to?"

Pierce turned towards Bosun, the dog was trembling in the doorway. "Where's the boy?" our leader asked.

My gagging stopped, "He got away. Even if we find this 'project' they'll be waiting there."

"Then we'll have to move fast," Pierce turned his gaze towards Stein.

The Construct-Creator nodded, he opened a panel on the back of Franky. The machine expanded, it's back opening further like the wings of a beetle. Stein took his Dwarven-Engine out of his tool belt and fitted it into the open cavity of the construct. The back opened even wider, and the redhead stepped up inside the construct. He slipped in and the back closed. The only part of the dwarf I could see was his eye poking out of the space left after he had removed the robot's eye previously.

In my peripheral I saw the panicking canine

jogging into the security room and staring intensely at one of the feeds. I was about to tell him that we need to hurry, but I saw his hackles rising up. A low growl became apparent, even over the loud alarms. I quickly walked over and looked at the screen.

Suddenly, Bosun nearly knocking me down ran snarling out of the room. Marsha yelled after him, as he headed out the door the orc guard had pointed out to Pennon. I glanced back at the screen, my skin crawled.

On the security stream labeled 'Lab', was what looked like a medical room. Several gurneys lined the back wall, only one person laid in one of the beds; a woman. My shoulders tensed; they had taken more than Gordon.

I swept my gaze to what appeared to be a hand truck with a metal canister the size of a refrigerator resting on it. I squinted at the canisters glass display window, my heart dropped into my stomach.

Inside the container I saw a young man's face.

SEVEN

FRANTICALLY, I took out my laptop and connected it to the security panel. I moved as quickly as I could to type in a simple code, setting off alarms throughout the facility. Subtle had already left the building, but the sensitivity of alarms allowed for a barrage of false information to the guards through which we could move. I pressed enter and left the computer in the room to continue running its script. Only one of the sequences of the alarms would actually represent intruders moving through the building, but all seven of them would look life it.

I shut the security room door, hoping I had earned us a little more time. I turned to the rest of the party and my nose recoiled as I saw the bodies splayed across the floor once again.

Pierce nodded to me and said, "What the hell is Bosun doing running off?

"He saw Gordon on one of the camera feeds," I said.

The leader took out the tablet and handed it to me, "Keep watch on the runaway, he'll likely lead others to us," he said.

With a wave of his hand, he motioned us all to move out. We sprinted through the door and headed down the hallway towards the lab. Pierce took the lead with both Stein and Marsha in tow behind him. Pennon, following them in turn, ripped off the jacket and uniform shirt, stripping down to the bandaging wrapped around his torso.

Already panting from the exertion, I tried my best to keep up. Stein's new robotic feet loudly clanked against the floor. We neared the upcoming right turn and I could hear approaching footsteps.

Stein edged towards the upcoming corner and pulled back his mechanical fist. Suddenly, two armed guards rounded the corner. Before either could visually register all of us, a large metal fist crunched into the chest of one of them. Loud snapping echoed past the wailing alarms, setting my teeth on edge.

The guard with the now-crumpled rib cage slapped against the far wall. Almost before he made contact, Stein grappled the other by the left leg. In a single motion, the mechanical man swung the guard around to gain momentum, then slammed him into the hallway corner. I glanced away from the broken body and looked down at the tablet.

Jackson's body-cam still showed him frantically sprinting down an empty hallway. I looked back up to see the others moving forward again. My ankles ached as I pushed onward, trying to catch up. Up ahead, I could see Bosun standing in front of the door to the lab, his hand grasping the doorknob.

Upon closer inspection, I noticed that the canine was using his strength to hold the door closed. We approached and Marsha stepped forward. Suddenly, a laser burst through the door and grazed the dog's cheek. He yelped and jumped back, the door swung open to reveal a laser-rifle-holding xenoform hyena guard.

I clenched my eyes shut and heard the hyena yell, followed by a loud bang. The smell of gunpowder wafted through the air. I opened my eyes to see Marsha, her gun smoking in her hands. A quiet gurgling sound came from inside the lab.

I tried to focus on only looking forward.

We entered the lab and I glanced at the florescent, light-covered ceiling, doing my best to not think about the sopping wet floor. I didn't want to look down and see the color of our footprints.

We filed in, Bosun and Pennon in the back, Glenmont's compatriots in the front. Just like the security feed I had seen earlier, medical gurneys lined the back wall of the room. Large medical equipment beeped and whirred all around us.

Two other doors exited the room, one in the middle of the wall across from the gurneys and the other to the right of the huge canister at the end of the room. My eyes flitted from the container holding the young man to the last gurney that held the woman. Time was short and I didn't know what to prioritize.

Bosun made my decision for me. He pressed past us, running up to the end of the room. He placed his hands on the canister's glass panel, pushed his nose to the glass, and emitted an agonizing whine. His ears drooped and his tail kept between his legs. Wrapping his bulky arms around the canister, squeezing his fingers into the tiny edges of the cylinders lid, he strenuously tried to open it like a desperately hungry man trying to open an oyster with naught but his bare hands.

The canine snarled with frustration as he flexed and strained in vain. His fingers slipped and he lost his grip, falling to the ground. The poor dog began to violently sob.

"Gordon!" Bosun rested his forehead against the glass, tears cascading down his face. "What have they done to yah?" his voice croaked.

His sorrowful face turned to rage, his eyebrows tightly knitting together and his ears pulling back. Suddenly, with an incensed howl he began to beat his fists against the canister, every swing punctuated by a muffled thud that reverberated across the room.

I ran to his side, placing a hand on Bosun's shaking back. He flinched at my touch, then let his clenched fists drop to his sides. I stepped an inch closer to the glass panel, my eyes became glued to the canisters displayed contents; the world went stark cold. My head reeled and my knees trembled, all life was replaced with abject horror.

On the security feed I had recognized a human face, but now I could see the rest of Gordon. And what I saw no longer came near what one would label 'human'.

Peering past the glare of the glass, my brain buzzed like it was filled with battery acid. Gordon's limbs, each arm up to the elbow, each leg up to the knee had wires and blackened metal weaved gruesomely into his reddened agitated flesh.

The flesh around the cybernetic implants was malformed and twisted, the normal smooth texture replaced with rough patches of infected cuts and scratches. The color a shade of grey pallor, the bruised skin sagged like the molted coat of an ill Shar-Pei dog. The portions of interlaced body and tech bubbled a little with orange puss, the only sign of color left on his flesh. My stomach acid rocketed up my esophagus with my disgust. I firmly held the puke in my mouth and swallowed it back down with much effort.

Pennon strode over to us with intense curiosity in his amber eyes, he looked at the man in the tube, then quickly looked away. His expression didn't change except for his eyes, they went duller in color and became less focused; disassociation is an understandable coping mechanism.

The hylathan stared blankly at the dog in despair, "We need to keep movin'."

The lizard's eyes flickered back to the canister, and his back suddenly went board-straight. Eyes shifted from dim brown back to a lava-like hue. With a sharp focus in his visage, he hissed. I followed his line of sight, my mind flashed back to the wretched nubs on his back I saw upon our first encounter.

In the dark, I first mistook them for shadow. But as my gaze followed Pennon's, I realized leathery, night-sky-colored wings protruded from Gordon's back, folded neatly behind him.

Pennon, enraged, swung his talons against the glass panel. My heart lifted for a moment remembering Glenmont's safe and the ease in which the reptilian had cut through it.

The claw points struck and scratched across the glass, the high-pitched nails-across-chalkboard sound pained my ears. Three long gash-like scratches were left, but it wasn't enough. The glass was reinforced and thick, not to mention Pennon didn't have any hylathan pheromones to boost his strength this time.

Bosun gave a pleading look to Stein and Marsha, "Use some o' yer magic!"

Marsha tried hiding her sad grimace with a look of steely confidence, it didn't work. Stein, even though all we could see of his face was one of his eyes, I perceived a pained expression in the corners of his eye.

Pierce turned to the construct-creator, "Where's the engine?"

Stein answered slowly, "It's... in that container."

The mechanized redhead pointed one of his metal enhanced arms towards Gordon. I whipped my head around to see for myself. All of the wires from those cybernetics moved...somewhere. Up to his torso. Right where Stein's finger pointed. I had done what Glenmont asked, I found his engine— right in the chest of a young man who hadn't deserved any of what had been done to him.

Bosun's eyes bulged with horror, "Get em' outta there!"

"Don't think you'll be able to," a frail voice responded.

All our heads snapped towards the voice, the final gurney. We laid eyes upon the woman and I felt a pang of distress. The brunette woman lay there in a hospital gown, connected to all manner of life-supporting machines. The word 'sickly' fell far short of adequately describing her decrepitude. She breathed sharply, her chest moving in jagged ups and downs.

Her brown hair in measly patches atop her head, her face blemished by the cruel contortions of experimentation. The right side of her body looked like a bulbous, bruised balloon about to pop. The formally tight skin on her left side now hung in pools around her skeletal bones. I stared in disbelief. Bosun let out a soft, frightened whine.

The woman wheezed for a moment, then spoke once more. "The alarms. They'll be here soon," she gasped for breath and then continued, "You need to go."

"No! We're not leaving em'," my furry friend argued.

Pennon nodded in agreement, "Just hack the damn thing," he said and pointed to the canister.

Stein shook his head, "Not enough time, that thing's made to have one set of controls for one person. Tricking it into believing that I have the only controls will take too long." I hadn't examined the code myself, but if this thing had some form of biometric lock...I gave Stein a nod, and sighed as I did.

"They're gonna take him outside today, that's why they have him packed in that can," the weak voice of the woman said.

Pierce looked at the woman, his steely glare not softening. "What's your part in this?"

The lady winced for a moment, then answered. "That boy and I, we make a good genetic match." Her head lulled to rest on her bloated shoulder, "There were others here, lucky-loos," she weakly lifted her skeleton hand to point to the other gurneys.

I counted the beds one by one, my brain rattled

the number inside my skull; twelve. Raising a hand to my mouth, I attempted to calm myself.

"They mutated our genes, frantically copying them over to that young man," she said. "Well... only the good ones," her eyes turned to the ceiling lights as she listed, "More strength, extreme temperature resistance, at this point he's only going to need to eat once a month."

"How do we get em' out?" cried Bosun.

The lady in the gurney tiredly shook her head, "You're not going to, here," she began a coughing fit, then her raspy breaths eased a little. "I can help you though."

Pierce's eyebrow raised, "How so?" he said.

Her eyelids looked heavy as she struggled to stay awake, "I heard where they're going to test him out." Her head drooped then started up for a moment, like she almost fell asleep. "If you promise, I'll tell you," she said, her voice turning into a pained yawn.

"Promise what?" I cautiously asked.

She gave me an agonizing smile, her eyes peacefully closed. "To kill me," she said cheerfully in her meek tone.

I recoiled back, and I began to clench my jaw. In that moment, the blackbox in my pocket began to vibrate. Jean was calling, I slipped my hand into my pocket and felt for the device. My fingertips rested on the item, but they felt no vibration. I was mistaken, the sensation was all in my head.

"I promise," Pennon whispered.

The woman's smile broadened, it was almost like a little color returned to her stark grey face.

"No," I said.

The lizard's head snapped to face me, "Don't have time to argue morality," he faced the woman once more. "Tell us."

I gripped my pistol tightly, "I said no!"

"Don't try me, old man," Pennon snarled. "I've got a job to do."

My mind raced back to the memory of warm, sunny days, filled with sunny smiles. I glanced at the mutilated woman, the many tubes connecting to her body from the daunting medical machines. The bright song filled Sunday, shattered and morphed into the frozen snow covered grave visitation. All in my mind's eye.

"You're not taking her," I raised my pistol towards the murderous lizard.

Suddenly, two metal hands wrapped around me from behind. Stein forcefully bent my arms inward and bound them to my chest with his mechanical strength. I tried to thrash myself free, but his hold was too tight.

"Please, we can save her. No one else needs to die," my eyes watered and I continued sputtering. "Please. Please," I choked on my pleading words.

I heard behind me the techno-dwarf say, "Forgive us, friend."

"We let her be and she'll only be tortured further," Marsha solemnly added.

I frantically looked at Bosun, he gave me a guilty look. His jowls hung in a depressed frown and his ears lay flat against his skull. His eyes flitted from me to Gordon, then he simply looked down at his feet.

The leader of Glenmont's compatriots stepped to the bedside of the woman, and leaned close to her. He brought his ear to her mouth, she began to slowly whisper into his ear. After a few moments she stopped and he nodded.

"Thank you, ma'am," Pierce calmly whispered.

The woman smiled, showing her brilliant white teeth. Out of her entire body, it was her smile that had been left unblemished. My face stung with the salty tears rolling down my cheeks. The lady grinned at Pennon expectantly, he stepped forward and knelt beside the great machines keeping her alive. He found the power lines and one by one cut them with his talons.

The devices whirred to a halt. Her jagged breaths eased to a slow stop then start rhythm, her eyelids fluttered closed. We watched as her breaths became shallower and shallower, her head leaned back comfortably. She smiled blissfully, mouthing something unintelligible.

Then, gone.

Stein slowly let me go, I slid down to the floor. My heart felt like a snapped piece of twine. I'd never wanted to repeat this, I'd never wanted to feel this way again. Yet here I was.

"It's time to go," Pierce said.

"We can't leave em'!" Bosun protested.

Pierce directed his steely eyes towards the canine, "We can't move him, and we need to notify others about what's about to happen." He turned his gaze to me, "If you don't want others to die, we need to go. Now."

Suddenly, the alarms halted their screeching. A strange dread filled the air with the silence. We all froze, glancing at one another. The alarm speakers popped with static for a moment.

A cool, mocking tone flowed out from the speakers, "Guests! Don't leave just yet, I haven't even set out the fine china."

Pierce's brow furrowed and he put out his hand to me. I grasped it and he helped me onto my feet.

"Show me the tablet," he whispered.

I quickly took the thing out and we looked at the screen. Jackson's body-cam had been removed, but his tracker was still active. He wasn't far behind the door across from the gurneys.

"By the way," the jeering voice continued. "Play nice, I'm not against breaking my own toys. That... what was it that dear departed Twelve called it? 'Can'?" The voice paused for a moment, as if waiting for an answer.

"That 'can' has all sorts of features," the voice chuckled, "One being, switching the current feed of morphine to neurotoxin."

Bosun's ears shot straight up in shock, his hackles raised and he growled, "Yah can't do that!"

"I very well can. We deal more here with a question of whether I *will*. You may be too much of a simpleton to comprehend your situation, but I'm sure your friends can attest to the fact that. You. Are. Fucked," The voice spat out venomously.

The canine flitted his eyes from me to Pierce, a hopeless rage seething behind his eyes. He raised, then lowered his hand in a motion telling Bosun to calm down. The dog huffed, then looked longingly at the unconscious Gordon. My heart ached for the poor Newfoundland. To possibly lose his brother after getting this close; to barely recognize your loved one when you find them—the pain is overwhelming. I shook my head mournfully.

The voice burst from the speakers again, "No use drawing things out further, I can't wait to meet you."

The speakers crackled as they powered off. We stood there, braced, for several agonizing moments. Marsha clicked a few of the canisters on her bandoleer, readying them for use. Stein widened his stance and raised his mechanical fists. Pierce readied his pistol. Bosun and Pennon quickly grabbed a couple empty gurneys and tipped them over in front of us for makeshift cover.

My knuckles turned white as I tightly gripped my pistol. I caught myself unconsciously grinding my teeth with suspense. I knelt in behind the makeshift cover, closest to Gordon in his canister.

Three loud knocks came from the door across from the gurneys. A muffled voice called out from behind the door, "Remember, play nice kiddos."

The door opened and too many guards to count streamed in, lining themselves up across from us with their laser rifles raised. Black uniform after black uniform, flowed in. Menacing faces, staring hungrily at the intruders.

I saw Jackson enter and stand at attention beside the doorway. His eyes flitted over us and quickly looked away, afraid to look any of us in the eye. And behind him...

I blinked incredulously. The human boy who followed the mercenaries in looked nothing like I imagined a Prince of Balil. An angelic, cherub-like face beamed at us. A golden aura surrounded the boy, embalming his bleach-blond hair and peach-colored skin in its light. His bright yellow eyes crinkled at the edges, as he smiled gracefully, dimpling his perfectly rosy and otherwise round cheeks.

He wore a bright blue kimono speckled with pink cherry blossoms over his thin frame. The fabric reached to the floor and the sleeves were so long the ends hung far below his hands, hiding every inch of skin below his willowy neck.

Unquestionably beautiful, but something nagged at the back of my mind. Something simply did not sit with his presentation, I squinted at his outfit. Kimonos are a popular item for festivals, my Jean once wore one to experience that ancient and nearly forgotten culture. She'd been so embarrassed, because—because she'd folded it wrong, at first. Because one only ever folded the thing left to right, unless one happened to be dead. Only the dead fold theirs...

This boy's kimono folded right to left, and my spine tingled as the meaning sunk in. The Balil Prince slowly glanced at me, what looked like a knowing smile across his plump, pouty lips.

He scanned his eyes across the room, his short curls bouncing as he excitedly fidgeted up and down. Settling his gaze on Pierce, he slightly bowed his head in greeting.

"What a ragtag group," he said. "Very quaint. I would have guessed that the Dr. Glenmont would only trust his own kind to return his engine," the boy giggled.

"But here you are, along with the very thief who stole it in the first place. Unexpected, but welcomed," he steered his eyes to ogle Pennon. "And I thought I missed my chance to pay my scaly rogue in full." The boy's lips parted to show off his brilliantly white teeth—including some eerily sharp-looking canines. "How...fortunate," he said, bringing one of the drooping sleeves in front of his mouth to stifle his laughter.

The hylathan bared his fangs and hissed in response.

The boy pointed at Gordon, "Do you like what I did with your contribution?"

The reptilian's whole body was tense, his fists tightly clenched. His fiery eyes were trying to burn holes into the Balil's skull.

The Prince huffed, "Boring lizard." He crept his stare slowly over to Bosun. "Little Jackson here told me all about you. I was surprised when he said Gordon had a hound for a brother," he looked the dog up and down. "It's unlikely you two are blood related, but I have to wonder? The idea that my precious Gordon could have sprung forth into this world from the womb of a bitch, what a fantastic reality we would be living in."

Bosun stared at his feet, his tail between his legs. His teeth clenched teeth behind his snarling mouth, his breaths were heaving, but he did nothing else. The boy tilted his head curiously, then sighed.

"What am I doing, expecting a reaction when I hold all the cards?" the Prince said to himself. "Such terribly bad manners of me. I suppose it's to do with my own boredom. Apologies, guests," he looked wistfully at Gordon, "I've only let you be seen, not heard. How selfish of-"

"Are you going to kill us or are you just going to talk for eternity?" Pennon interrupted coldly.

The boy's face seemed to grow dark for a moment, then he returned to his sunny demeanor.

"You're right, I'll hurry this up. Some of us have appointments to keep and as Twelve told you I'm taking Gordon for a test drive," the boy beamed with pride.

"Exciting stuff," he said, as he fidgeted a little more. He waved at the canister and it began to roll forward.

Bosun stepped towards the canister to grasp at it, but every laser rifle snapped to aim at the canine. The Newfoundland froze in place, as Gordon left his reach through the door he'd been resting beside. The furry one's mouth was agape, his eyes frantically scanned the room for options.

I knew this was the end of the road. I cautiously reached into my pocket and shakily put on the experi-sense kit to my face. The boy's vantage was so locked on Bosun's expression of despair, he either didn't notice or care. With a press of a button, I began recording.

It was hopeless, but what else am I supposed to do? I'm nothing compared to my companions. If anyone was dying here, it was me. The old man. All I had to lose...was Jean.

The prince panned his view over all of us again, my entire body trembled when his wasp-colored eyes passed over me. He smirked.

"Twelve *was* a chatty-kathy wasn't she? Jackson?" the son of Balil queried the young mercenary.

Jackson flinched, then straightened his back, "Yes, sir!"

I didn't see the motion. One moment, Jackson stood at attention, waiting for an order from his Prince. The next...a thin, blackened, razor-sharp hand protruded from his back and glistened with his blood. The corners of the Prince's mouth were turned inhumanly upwards, contorting his face into a hyperbolic, yet surreal, expression of sick joy. The kimono sleeve now looked comically shorter than the revealed arm.

I held my breath. The impaled man's eyes went wide with shock and streams of vital fluids drained from the sides of his mouth. He turned his panicked expression towards me, but I could only stare back. I heard Bosun retch and loudly whine, heard Pennon hissing, Stein and Marsha gasping. The first sign of rage came from Pierce; he was breathing hard, almost growling.

"Look at me, Jack," The prince calmly commanded, and twisted his arm a little. The merc grunted and coughed with pain, splattering the kimono with red. "How did they find this place, hmm?"

The man curled forward and vomited velvet bile across the floor. He shook violently, all color drained from his complexion. His breathing became erratic and his eyes blank, he uselessly tried to push away from the arm with his limp hands.

The Prince's eyes went half-lidded with annoyance, "You're going into shock," he sneered sarcastically. "How very plain. I do hope the rest of your friends show better sport."

I could feel myself hyperventilating, my head going hazy. I couldn't control the rapid beating of my old heart, did Jackson deserve this?

Deep within, I answered myself: *no one deserves this.*

The boy-Prince lowered his arm, allowing the

convulsing body to slide sloppily off. Jackson slumped onto the floor in a pool of himself, clumsily twitching and jerking his hands and feet so they slipped across the cement, lubricated by his own blood. It was like he was attempting to create a gruesome snow angel.

My head wobbled with vertigo-like dizziness, my eyes couldn't comprehend this tragic Rorschach inkblot. All sound around me began to echo. I could hear Bosun vomiting. My entire perspective narrowed down to some foreboding tunnel.

The Prince spun around and walked though the door he had sent Gordon. Through the tightening keyhole of my vision I watched the door shut. Only a moment after Marsha must have thrown one of her canisters, because a bright flash blinded me. This was all followed by yelling and gunshots reverberating like ripples through the darkness of my mind.

Then it all faded away.

...

My hand waited patiently for me to command it to turn the doorknob, I stood there in the dim light, blankly staring at the wood finish. This is my home, yet I'm afraid to enter. I felt callous for feeling this way, but what had made this a home was slowly fading and I couldn't take it.

Coward, I scolded myself and turned the knob. The door creeped open to reveal my black and white boston terrier sitting by the door, welcoming my arrival. He jumped onto his feet and trotted over to me, looking up at me with his large eyes. I knelt down and scratched his ear, his eyes closed in relaxed response, he leaned into my hand.

Stopping for a moment, he opened his eyes to gaze up at me, he huffed and whined a little. His eyes were shiny with watery rims, if a dog could cry he was doing so. He was far more open and honest with his take on the situation than me. I patted his head.

"Thanks for watching over my Jean, Maxwell," I whispered to the pup.

He huffed again in response and rubbed his face into my hand.

I stood up and removed the package from my jacket pocket. Across from me was the bedroom, the door was ajar and dim light flooded out from the opening. I hated myself for dreading taking the few steps forward to see Jean. I rapped my knuckles against my forehead, hoping that the dull thud against my skull would knock some sense into me.

With a heavy sigh I headed for the bedroom.

Passing through the doorway I heard, "There you are, Martin."

"Sorry, I just had to pick something up," I said and held up the package.

I looked up at my wife, she was lying in bed with a book in her lap. She picked up the novel and set it down on the bed stand beside her. She smiled sweetly at me, but her eyes expressed confusion. It broke my heart that she felt she had to pretend that she understood.

"I was worried about where you disappeared to," she said.

I walked over and sat on the bed next to her. I lifted her hand and kissed it. As I lowered her hand,

I glanced at the book she had been reading. The bookmark hadn't moved in weeks, how many times has she read the same page?

I looked into her eyes. Over the course of her illness they had grown dimmer. She cheerfully looked at me, then her vision was drawn to the box in my hand.

"Oh, a package? When did you get that?" she asked.

I began to open the box, I pulled out a pouch. I unwrapped the black, quarter-sized circle and applied it to Jean's cheek.

Jean giggled, "What is this?"

"It's an experi-sense kit, it will record everything going on in that beautiful brain of yours," I explained. "Thoughts, memories, emotions...anything." I continued setting up the recording devices on her.

"Oh," she feigned comprehension.

Finally, I brought out the Black Box and plugged it into the kit. She watched closely, as I clicked a button and the light on the Black Box blinked.

"With a press of a button," she hummed.

"Any problem can be solved," I said.

...

As the months passed like sand being pulled into the sea, I watched the light in my Jean's eyes fade even further. I spent every moment caring for her, she slowly lost her ability to walk. Slowly she lost her ability to form more than a single sentence.

One day, I turned to her and saw her crying, her expression unchanged except for the tears dripping from her chin. I sprinted to her side and held her head. Wiping her eyes dry, I asked, "Why are you crying?"

Weakly, she brought her hand to her face, then looked at me. "I'm crying?" she said.

My sadness felt as though it had calcified and sat upon my heart, weighing down on every beat. "No, no, not at all. We were just having a great time," I comforted her.

"Yes, we were," The corners of her mouth twitched upward in a meek smile.

I leaned forward to kiss her forehead, so I could hide the tears lining my eyes from her view.

Many years of society's technological advancement meant everything from flying cars to advanced AI. Alzheimers, though, remained unconquered. We could grow entire organs in a tube to replace defective parts and extend a person's life, but the brain could not be physically recreated.

So, I went with the next best thing, I never had to say goodbye. I never had to accept that she was gone, she could live with me forever in this little Black Box.

EIGHT

THE MOVING floors roused me from my unconsciousness, pain shot through my skull. My head must have hit the cement hard when I fainted. Slowly, I gained more awareness of my surroundings. Muffled yelling beat at my eardrums and I realized that I was being dragged by the back of my jacket.

I opened my eyes and looked up. Bosun had a hold of me. His ears were pressed down flat and his left side was bleeding, with his free hand he grasped around his waist at his wound.

Looking back, I saw Pennon limping after us, a bullet-wound in his left thigh. More yelling sought after us and the lizard whipped around, his pistol at the ready. A few trigger pulls left afterburn images bursting in my vision. I blinked a few times, trying to fix my sight.

Opening my eyelids again, I saw Marsha and Stein following. The normally jolly redhead was covered in scorch marks, gashes, and laser holes. I couldn't tell how much of the damage was to Stein instead of Franky, but I hoped for the best. Marsha's hair was wild, tangled, and singed, but she looked otherwise uninjured.

She lobbed another canister towards the enemy fire, lasers burst forth in return. Stein strafed in front of the shots to guard Marsha with his mechanical body. Then the canister blew, slamming into my still-groggy eardrums and filling the air with a wave of heat and force. Bright, hot light filled the edges of my sight as a massive fire erupted in the wake of the blast.

My shoes skidded across the cement and bumped around as we began to ascend a metal ramp. We passed Pierce, waving us along, the reptilian limping not far ahead of him.

"Marsha, toss me a grenade," our leader called out.

Stein and Marsha closed the distance and she complied, chucking Pierce one of the last canisters on her bandoleer.

"Hold them off for as long as you can, help should be here soon. Don't let them take us down and if you can, survive!" the steely officer said.

The two of them saluted and faced the oncoming guards. Bosun pulled me into a dimly lit room and finally realized we were on a ship. Bosun let me go to lean against one of the black metal walls and desperately pant. Pennon limped inside and looked at the ship's controls.

"Don't know how to fly a Balil cruiser," the limping lizard said.

Pierce sprinted in and took the vehicle's steering yoke, "I do."

With a lurch, the ship lifted up and the ramp began to close, I was feeling strong deja vu. My eyes could finally focus. I could see the many black figures heading towards us and I could hear the lasers bouncing off the hull of the ship. Marsha and Stein held their ground. I didn't know if I'd ever see them again, and the thought cast a palor over my already-dismal mind. They were good people, and better soldiers.

It should have been me.

The ramp latched closed and the last of the facility's light disappeared from view. Only the eerie, yellow-tinted luminescence of the inside of the Balil ship cabin remained. At this point the color yellow made me sick, I never thought I'd miss the red interior of Pennon's ship.

I felt the ship launch out of the facility and rush for the planet's atmosphere with a powerful burst forward. The lizard began picking through the cabin's many compartments, shifting their contents around and frowning in disgust. Pushed to the far back of the furthest compartment from the driver's controls the lizard pulled out a dusty medical kit.

My head buzzed as I spoke, "A med-kit? They have necromantic tech to fix any damage to their bodies."

Pennon glared at the kit, "Kept around for mercenaries and prisoners, I'd guess."

The lizard walked over to Bosun. The big canine had his head pressed to the wall and his eyes clenched shut in pain. With gentleness I could never have expected from the scaly rogue, he began to tend to the dog's wound on his side. Pressing a cotton pad firmly over the dripping wound and then securing it with a wrapping around the waist.

"Thanks," Bosun grunted.

"Anyone else bleeding other than me?" Pennon asked.

No one answered him, "Good," the Hylathan said, then began dressing the laser hole in his thigh.

The ship's walls shook violently. We felt a few jolts pass as we passed through Altay's atmospheric layers. Pierce took a hold of what looked like the radio as we once more entered the edge of space. He flicked a few switches and frantically spoke into the receiver.

"Mayday, mayday, mayday. This is a distress call from a commandeered sons of Balil aircraft. I repeat, this is a commandeered sons of Balil aircraft. This is Officer Pierce, do you read me starport? Over." he said.

I could hear static over the radio, then it clicked. "This is starport, Officer Pierce. We read you. Security forces already en route to the ore testing facility. Over." a voice responded.

"Good, I have two guys still down there. Over." Pierce said.

The radio crackled, "Do you require recovery from your current position? Over."

"No, we are chasing down a class-three threat. We have acquired info that the sons will be attacking in Orc Frontier space on Planet Sixteen, Tribe Of The Sunken Palms. Over." the leader said.

"We'll try to warn the tribe of the danger and will send help as soon as possible. Over," The voice said.

"Copy. Pursuit continuing. Officer Pierce out." Our leader flipped off the radio and returned his focus to piloting the ship.

Pennon finished bandaging his leg, "How do you know how to drive this thing?"

Pierce sighed, "I've fought the Balil before, years ago."

The lizard's eyebrows shot up, "You kill any?"

The officer smirked, "A few."

"What stopped you?" I asked wryly, still sitting firmly on the floor.

He grimaced and glanced at me. "If it was easy to kill those bastards, they wouldn't exist. I lost so many friends combating them...well, there aren't many of us still breathing to train the new ones."

Bosun turned around and eased himself next me, wincing as he sat down. "There a special way tah off em'?"

"Their outside's just a shell,' said Pierce. "What's inside is what matters. They have this... orb, in their bodies. Crystal, it looks like. When they risk dying, the orb attempts to open a portal to escape into. Shatter it before it gets away and you just killed yourself a son of Balil." Pierce said.

I noticed the crack in my glasses and I thought of something important. "When you used that- that 'loud' bullet in our first gunfight."

The leader nodded his head, "You're smart Martin, I'm glad you noticed that." He stretched his shoulders back, then relaxed them. "Means you didn't completely lose your mind back there. Yes... sonic attacks I've found to work very well on Balil."

I thought for a moment, then said, "The spell on the bullet creates a soundwave?"

The Arcane-Gunman gave me a thumbs up, "Yup. Crystalline structures have difficulty withstanding the resonance—sorry about your glasses, by the way."

"Then why didn't you use it? We just watched that bastard walk away." Pennon said.

"It's not so easy that a simple pull of the trigger would have solved everything. The blast of the sound must be as close as possible to the orb, which...well, who knows where in the body it resides. If I miss, he realizes how much of a threat I really am—at which point I end up like Jackson. Nothing will get you killed faster than being a threat," Pierce said.

"We coulda' done something to get Gordon," Bosun whimpered.

"He didn't outright kill us himself because he underestimated us. We amused him, but we didn't threaten him. That leaves this as our best course of action," Pierce said.

"But what are we going to do once we get to the Orc Frontier?" I asked.

The sole remaining techno-dwarf squeezed the steering yoke tighter, "We'll cross that bridge when we get there," he said, his eyes fixed forward.

Pennon rolled his eyes, "If the bridge hasn't already burned down."

The large canine sniffled like he was about to cry again. The hylathan looked a little guilty and put a hand on the dog's shoulder.

"We'll figure this out." The lizard consoled.

"How soon will we make it there?" I asked.

Pierce pinched the bridge of his nose and thought for a moment, "At the speeds this thing can go...maybe an hour?"

"Then punch it," Pennon said.

Our leader nodded and pushed up the throttle. The hull creaked and we felt a jolt as we burst forward even faster. Instead of a front window, there was a screen display in front of Pierce. The stars streaked by immeasurably fast. It donned on me how far this investigation had come and where it was likely going. At least I still had my Jean, I thought, absently touching the experi-sense detector on my face.

Slowly, I got to my feet and walked to the back of the ship. My friends gave me curious looks, but didn't say anything.

I pulled out the Black Box and opened my feed to Jean. Like an echo through the icy tundra, her voice crackled through the speakers. "Martin, I was worried," she sighed.

"I know, honey. I'll be done with this job soon," I said.

"I missed you," She said.

I fiddled with the zipper on my jacket, "Soon, I'll likely have all the time in the world for you my love."

She giggled, "Good, I miss you."

I smiled, but it felt hollow. "I miss you too, just wait for me a little while longer. I'll be home soon, one way or another."

"I will," Jean said.

I imagined her freckled sun-kissed arms and the spark in her eyes on those hot summer days. "I love you," I whispered.

"Ditto," she laughed.

I turned off the speaker and let her rest back into the ether of the Black Box's programming.

Disconnecting Jean from my feed, I turned back around and sat next to my party members again.

Pennon looked me up and down slowly, "Can I be honest?"

"I'm guessing not," I said with a corner of my mouth crinkling upwards. It's not often somebody serves up a straight line like that.

The lizard sighed with frustration, "I'm being serious here, buddy."

"This situation is already pretty serious," I said, removing my glasses to look at them nonchalantly. I didn't feel like opening up to anyone right now.

"All the more reason to be honest," the Hylathan said. "I don't think that device of yours is doing you any favors."

Taking a deep breath in and then out, I calmly responded, "Please, you don't know what you're talking about."

The reptilian sighed, "Fine." He turned his head towards Bosun, "Tell me about you and your brother."

The canine's ears shot up in surprise, "Yah don't really wanna hear about that, do yah?"

Rolling his eyes once more, the lizard said, "No, I have a hole in my thigh that hurts like a bitch and I want to pass the time. Humor me."

Nervously fidgeting with his hands, twirling his thumbs over each, other the furry one said, "We're not blood. Balil was right about that. Don't remember much o' life before knowin' him, other than it was much harder." He smiled at the recollection as he spoke. "Lived in a-rough and tumble kinda situation, just tryin' to survive. He would steal fer me, throw fists fer me. I was small back then, couldn't help myself." Flexing his muscular arm proudly he laughed, "Then I sorta' exploded. Always hoped I'd grow strong, gonna pay Gordon back and more. I'm gonna be the big brother for a change."

His smile dropped, "Turns out, muscles don't make a lotta' money unless yer willing to beat others over the head. So, Gordon kept doing tech trials." He pointed a thick index finger to the side of his skull, "His mind is stronger than mine, he can handle that stuff."

The dog's ears drooped down, "I wished fer the wrong thing, shoulda' wished fer smarts."

Pierce piped up, "You'll sing a different tune when you beat that Balil within an inch of his life."

Bosun nodded, his eyes burned with intense determination.

Pennon tried to hide a smile, but he couldn't disguise the fact that the canine was growing onto him. Slowly but surely, the hairy lug had gained our friendship. It was hard not to like such a genuine soul.

"ETA?" the lizard asked.

"Twenty minutes," answered the officer.

The scaly rogue let out a frustrated sigh.

"What about you, Pennon?" I asked.

The lizard brought his arms akimbo and tilted his head, "What about me?"

"You made a deal with Glenmont, about your daughter," I said.

Idly scratching his scaly neck the reptilian said, "So you want me to spill my guts, when you can just clam up?"

Rolling my eyes, I said, "Just trying to help you pass the time."

Pennon snarled, "You're not trying to help anyone, Bosun wants to rescue Gordon, I want to secure a safe future for my little girl, what the hell are you here for?"

My eyebrows shot up in surprise of this sudden confrontation, "Glenmont's engin-"

"Bullshit!" The lizard cut off my answer. "What kind of relationship with the doctor do you have that makes you willing to die for his engine?"

I glanced at Bosun, he was flitting his eyes nervously between the two of us.

"Well, I also want to help Gordon," I said, turning my gaze towards those bright reptilian amber eyes.

Pennon scowled deeply, "Liar," he pointed one of his razor sharp claws in my direction. "You are here for one reason only, and that's you see an opportunity to finally die yourself. It's all you want, out of this."

A pit began to grow in my stomach, "Like I said, you don't know what you are talking about." I crossed my arms over my chest, almost subconsciously, as if to guard myself.

"You act as if we have no clue what you keep in your pocket, but do you really think we're that brainless?" the Hylathan asked. "Only people who want to die talk to those things."

I stared daggers at the lizard, "Shut your mouth," I warned.

The reptilian threw his arms out to his sides angrily, "Or what? You'll point your gun at me again?"

"That woman didn't need to die," I said. I felt heat building in my chest.

Pennon shook his head in disagreement, "You would've allowed her to suffer to save your feelings?"

I stammered back, "Of course not!"

"Cool it, you two," Pierce called out, "We're here."

I peered at the screen, a ball of green covered in plum colored clouds was expanding in front of us. In a matter of seconds we approached the planet's atmosphere and the ship began to shake. The officer steering the ship would periodically look down at the many gauges and displays, calculating where and how to land.

Our destination appeared at last, at first just a bright orange speck glowing in front of us, but ever-growing. The closer we came, the brighter the reds and yellows ahead grew. We were finally getting low enough to the ground to see the many mountain ranges, lakes and rivers that snaked across the landscape.

The ship passed through the hazy mist of a purple cloud, momentarily hiding the scenic views. Finally bursting forth, pulling pieces of cloud along with us, we could see. Bosun and Pennon jumped up and stood beside me, observing the scene before us.

We stood there, gawking at what was below in shock. Fire engulfed the Tribe of the Sunken Palms. Orcs ran to and fro in panic, attempting to quell the flames or escape. My heart leapt into my throat. I could see the misshapen forms of corpses scattered across the smoke-choked tribe.

Gordon's test had already begun, and we were too late.

I frantically searched to find the source of the attack, on the other side of the burning cabins and huts a large plume of flame popped up, followed by more. I pointed it out to Pierce and he steered around the destruction, finding ourselves on the opposite end of the tribe.

A large horde of huge orc warriors surrounded an epicenter of carnage. Small explosions raged through the ranks of battle-hardened fighters. In the middle of this struggle stood Gordon.

Pierce landed the ship on the grassy hill below us, a safe distance from the quarrel. The ship's ramp began to lower and with that the soundproofing of the hull was canceled. The loud cracking of burning wood and clay reached our ears, along with the gut-wrenching screams of the survivors below.

The moment the ramp hit the ground, Bosun jumped out of the ship and onto the green knoll. The hylathan followed and I watched as Pierce readied his rifle. He slipped the grenade Marsha had tossed him into one of his tactical pouches. Together, we ran into the strangling smoke and chaos.

From atop the rounded hill we tried to make out Gordon among the struggling green and gray bodies. Blood and sweat was palpable in the ashen air. When the orcs notice us, would they consider us enemies? If we took action, would we kill Gordon? A giant, looming cloud rolled over the village, darkening every inch of the conflict.

With great force, a warrior flew back, thrown from the fight. He landed with a spine-shattering crack upon the blackened soil. More fighters joined him, thrown from the focal point of the battle as a few moments passed. The air seemed to electrify for a second and I instinctively looked up.

The cotton-candy cloud above swirled and wafted away as it was disturbed, the condensed mists revealing a slowly creeping, gargantuan ship. The Prince's personal transportation.

The ship shifted and waved like a shadowy mirage. It gave the impression of a dark, crawling, rotten octopus. Only the sons of Balil could design such a nightmarish vehicle.

A voice echoed from the heavens, that same childish voice that had mourned the ease of Jackson's death. "That's no way to win. Do it right!"

A whirring, winding up noise responded to the voice, it made my skin prickle with goosebumps. I turned my head towards the new racket and saw a glowing orange light growing brighter in the center of the chaos. I had no idea what was happening, but a cold sweat ran down my spine and the hair on the back of my neck stood on end.

A small, almost inconsequential murmur replaced the warrior's yells as the field fell silent. The many struggling bodies froze for a single moment, staring in confusion. Then the whirring halted. The crackling flames filled the air, but we may have just as well been surrounded by silence with the sheer amount of anticipation. A high whimper escaped Bosun's muzzle.

My old ears pricked up a little, the remnants of ancient instincts firing off in adrenalinized bursts. My senses focused in, straining to determine what was about to happen. The sound of tearing flesh and a single man's scream suddenly ripped through the still air.

Then, like the crack of a whip, the screaming snapped off and the tearing stopped along with it. Incensed cries erupted from the orcs collectively lurching forward in a frantic attack. Through all the weapon swinging arms, I could only see this orange glow slowly turning into a hot white.

The glow moved, and started whirring once more. Like tires rolling through sloshed snow, the sounds of flesh being torn, muscles rent, and bones being ground into marrow covered paste washed over me. Distorted forms toppled to the ground, twitching dismembered limbs rolled around like they wanted to escape.

The previous rebellious cries became indescribable groans and wails as the orc tribe's numbers shrank. As their bodies fell, we saw the source of the calamity. Stumbling through the carnage, a wide-eyed, panicking Gordon uncontrollably windmilled his cybernetic arms, collapsing anyone who opposed him. Blood draped his body like a thin velvet sheet.

In his chest glowed the engine, the source of the light. The device stuffed into his body was running so hot the metal glowed white and the blood around it boiled and steamed. The young man grimaced with each throw of his fists, tears streaming down his face.

A warpaint-covered green orc sprinted forward and swung his battleax at the young man's head. I blinked as Gordon stopped the blade with a single cybernetic hand. Blackened metal fingers wrapped around the edge of the blade. Gordon's altered body stood frozen, his head the only piece of him trembling violently.

"Go on," the Prince's voice boomed from the looming ship above.

The orc struggled to yank the weapon from Gordon's grasp, but the Balil's pet project shook his head. His unblinking eyes shifted all around him, only stopping momentarily to gaze at the scattered death he had left at his feet. Lower lip quivering, he continued to shake his head in disobedience.

Bosun began to step forward.

"This is no time for rebellion, my precious Gordon," the Prince's voice rained down on our ears.

The young man's whole body quaked in response.

Gordon automatically pulled back on the axe. The orc lurched forward, bringing his skull into range of Gordon's free, metallic hand. The punch connected with mechanical force. The poor orc's head erupted like a watermelon stuffed with explosives.

Bosun stopped in his tracks, mouth agape in shock at his brother.

The headless corpse stood there still holding tightly to its weapon, Gordon let go of the blade and the corpse dropped. The warriors still left alive cowered back and glanced at one another for guidance.

One by one, they decided to flee, sprinting as fast as their legs could carry them to some unknown destination. I looked at my companions. Pennon seemed split; his body cringed back, but his eyes burned almost as bright as the Dwarven Engine ahead of us.

Pierce crouched on one knee and readied his rifle, aiming it straight at Gordon's quivering form. Bosun looked back with a frightened expression, shaking his head at the techno-dwarf. The leader solemnly nodded back, and motioned the canine to move forward.

Gordon hadn't noticed us yet, his head was shivering as he gaped at the ground around him. His metal fists clenched tighter and began to shake erratically.

An inhuman screech pierced my mind. Reflexively, I put my hands over my ears in a vain attempt to block the sound an out of tune violin with battered vocal cords for strings amplified a hundred times over.

And coming from Gordon's mouth.

Cautiously stepping towards his brother, Bosun closed the distance between them. The canine stopped two yards from the howling man, his open palmed hands up in front of him in a calming gesture. Pennon lingered several feet away, watching carefully.

In a soft calming tone the dog spoke, "Brother, I'm here."

Gordon's wailing cut off suddenly. Slowly he lifted his eyes, to stare entrancingly at the familiar Xenoform. The corner of his mouth twitched up into a hopeless half smile. Bringing a blood-soaked hand to his face he covered his eyes.

A mournful voice croaked from Gordon's ragged throat, "N-no, I don't see." He wrapped his free arm tightly around his head, pressing his metallic fingers into his shaggy brown hair then tightly grasping the strands. He was trying to contain himself, "Brother... please, don't let me see."

Bosun took a step closer, tears lined the rims of his eyes. He gulped down his sorrow, pretending that he was all right. "Time to go," he said, and he kept his voice calm and level as he extended a hand to his brother.

An otherworldly chuckle cascaded from Gordon's lips. The sound rang familiar in my ears, the same tone and inflection as the Prince's sneering cackle. Gordon struggled for a moment, shaking his head, then his own voice returned to his lips for a moment.

"Leave, you dumb mutt," the young man said to his brother, his voice gentle with concern.

The canine's ears shot up and his tail wagged a little, sensing the care in his brother's voice. "I'll protect yah," he said.

Another burst of static filled the air above us. The monstrous ship closed the distance between it and the ground a little further. The Prince's voice boomed over us, "This is touching, I suppose. But I find it tiresome. End this reunion, my pet."

The altered man's whole body quaked, but he stayed put. He clenched his eyes closed and began muttering to himself repeatedly, "Can't, can't, can't, can't."

My furry friend took several steps closer. Now only a few feet away from his brother, he kept his hand outstretched and his smile steady. Pennon tentatively inched himself nearer as well. I glanced anxiously at Pierce; his eye remained on his rifle's scope.

"Do you want to disappoint me?" The Balil's voice echoed down to us.

The muttering became a broken cry of, "Can't! Can't! Can't!"

Bosun brought himself even nearer, then placed his hands on Gordon's shoulders. "Fight em'," the dog said with a pained smile.

The man's cries morphed into confident refusals, "I won't! I won't!"

"YOU WILL!" The Prince screamed petulantly.

Like lightning had just struck the brothers, they began to howl and painfully convulse. Bosun continued to hold tightly to Gordon's shoulders. Their muscles wildly tensed and relaxed, reminiscent of an epileptic fit. They cried our together as the Prince tortured them from afar for their disobedience.

And then, the whirring sound began again. Jerkily, Gordon lowered the hand from over his eyes, closed it into a fist, and pulled back. My heart skipped a beat, I stepped forward lifting my gun. Pennon sprinted towards the two brothers.

The cybernetic fist launched towards Bosun's stomach. My trigger finger twitched, but I refused to pull. I didn't want to kill anyone.

Pennon leapt for the dog, shoulder checking him out of the way. My ears cringed and I choked on my own breath, as Gordon's fist tore through the hylathan's torso. The lizard slipped back, losing his balance. A stream of velvet sprayed across the young man and Pennon's limp form slumped to the ground.

Bosun sat up from the damp soil, his ears

flattened and his lips pulled back in a snarl. A low growl passed through his clenched fangs, sloppy tears dripped from his shock struck eyes.

I heard Pierce fire, and a loud ping reverberated. Gordon's arm had moved to block the bullet, lightning-fast. I lowered my firearm—useless, now. My fingers went numb and I dropped the pistol.

I gawked at this monstrosity, his mad gaze being obscured by Pennon's blood steaming off of him. The continually darkening smoke seemed to gather round him, like bad memories that never let you forget. The threatening whirs emitting from his body made my teeth chatter.

Slowly, he turned his head to look at Bosun who was laying there in disbelief, resting on the ashes of this tragic tribe.

The Prince's voice returned, "I'm inspired! Gordon, come back here."

"Wait," Bosun choked.

Pennon's dark wings unfolded to their full length from Gordon's back, "Don't let me see you," Gordon warned, his own voice back in control once more.

Bosun clawed towards his brother. Before he could reach him, his leathery wings powerfully beat and the Prince's toy lifted off the ground. He flapped his way to the welcoming tendrils of the ship above us and disappeared into that grotesque, floating abyss.

The cheerful voice of the Prince hailed us, "Bring that stolen ship and yourselves up here soon. I do so hope you haven't decided to call it quits; that would be all too disappointing."

Pierce and I glanced at one another. The sound of labored coughing tore my focus to Pennon. Frantically, I ran to his side and pulled the experi-sense kit from my pocket.

His face convulsed with pain as his wounds poured blood. More fluid flowed out from the sides of his mouth. I fell to his side. With trembling fingers, I began to shakily apply the experi-sense kit to his clammy face.

He weakly tried to wave me away, but I persisted. With the little strength he had left he angrily ripped off the device and threw it at me, snarling.

"Don't make me a twisted copy!" Pennon said.

I looked at the gaping hole in his chest, "I don't think you're going to make it," I shakily argued.

He coughed again, "You think?"

Bosun crawled over and lifted the lizard's head to rest more comfortably on his knees.

"Thanks," the hylathan said and grimaced as he took a jagged breath.

"Pennon, what about your girl?" I sniffled, putting forward a strong face. "You can still be there for her."

"No," he smirked weakly "The thing you'd make would only cast a shadow, hold her back. You can't grow, clinging on like that. That isn't the point of all this," His eyes began to flutter closed and his amber iris' began to dim.

"The point of what?" I whimpered, losing control of my crying.

He smiled toothily, and for the first time I saw through the lizard's hardened exterior. Those smoldering eyes stared back into mine. Then he turned his gaze to Bosun, the dog he'd just met a day or so ago. "Pennon" had been nothing more than the name of my suspect...now it was the name of a friend. A friend who'd given his life for Bosun's.

His voice came out breathy and slow, "Living."

Bosun held Pennon's head and his shoulders shook with grief, teardrops splashed across the hero's scales as the fire in those magma-like eyes turned to coal.

I felt Pierce's hand on my shoulder, squeezing. Bringing me back to this devastated world. I turned to look at him, at eye level now that I was on my knees.

"I know you two aren't used to mourning a lost comrade. It's a hard thing to learn to do quickly." he sighed, then glanced upwards. "But we've got work to do."

I followed his gaze, lifting my head to the ship hanging above us. The grief weighing on my heart transformed into a burning rage. Glaring down that flying, cancerous thing through the tears still hanging in my eyes I said, "You're right. We shouldn't disappoint."

NINE

PENNON'S BODY rested limply in Bosun's arms as
we considered what to do next. I glanced up at the
floating terror above us, then to the smoldering
village remnants.

"We can't take him with us," I said.

The canine looked at me in shock, "Can't just
leave em'."

Pierce turned his steely gaze to the ship above
us, "He's right. If we fail and we have him with us,
they'll cut him into bits and use every little piece."

"And they won't do that to us?" The furry one
asked.

"They'll get less use out of us," I answered, as I
stooped to pick up my pistol.

Bosun sniffled a little and looked down at
Pennon's meditative face, "Then what do we do?"

Pierce looked to the last of the flames, "Give
him a warrior's funeral," he said.

...

Covered in soot and ashes, we trudged up the

hill and into the ship. We closed the ramp and watched the screen display of Pennon's pyre. Its fire reached high into the air, almost as though he waved goodbye. I felt my grief flooding up my chest to bring tears to my eyes, I closed them. The ship began to rise, I kept my eyelids shut.

I didn't want to look at the rotten octopus we were flying into. I didn't want to see its taunting tendrils welcoming us inside, its beak opening wide to consume us. I gripped the Black Box tightly, allowing only the camera on my glasses to observe the treacherous nature of our situation.

Somehow, we were going to save Gordon. That's all I wanted to think about.

Pierce landed inside the Balil ship's open hangar, then quickly turned to us. "Don't go gung-ho. We want to get as close as possible to the Prince." He cocked his pistol, muttering his spell into the magazine. "The bastard wants to toy with us, so there's a chance he lets us. If we kill him, maybe we can calm down Gordon."

I watched the officer hide Marsha's grenade and another enchanted magazine under his tucked shirt, then put his pistol in the holster at his side.

The ramp began to lower without our command, below were nine guards pointing laser rifles at us. We raised our open hands in surrender and slowly stepped down the ramp. I looked around the hangar, the same yellow lighting against black reinforced steel.

Every time my eyes moved something in my peripherals squirmed. It was like the Prince's ship was alive, it wouldn't be hard to believe all things considered.

When we came down to the guard's level, one demanded, "Hand over those pistols, they won't do you any good anyway."

Bosun and I looked to Pierce, he nodded for us to comply. Pierce unholstered his gun and slapped it into one of the guard's waiting palms. A moment later, the big dog and I did the same.

"Come this way," one of the black-clad guards said, then began to lead us out of the hangar.

My eyes flickered to Pierce's torso. We just had to hope there was no pat down. I saw Bosun paw a little at the bandages wrapped over his side, his eyes unfocused as he absentmindedly followed along.

We were lead through a set of doors and continued down a twisting corridor. An elevator opened and we stepped inside. Surrounded by mercenaries, the elevator jolted and soon after we began ascending.

Standing awkwardly with enemies on all sides, the yellow hue around us flickered with every floor passed. The bulkiest guard to my right loudly cleared his throat, I accidentally flinched in response.

The guard's eyes snapped to look at me with his eyebrows up in surprise, "Oh, sorry," he said.

Another guard elbowed him in the side, shaking his head in disapproval of his comrade. The guard who cleared his throat looked embarrassed. Color raced to his face, turning his cheeks and ears red. He then straightened his back and looked ahead, focusing now on the elevator doors.

The elevator slowed to a stop and I focused back onto the task at hand. Sliding open, the doors revealed a large hallway with windows lining the right wall. Striding forward, I turned my head towards the windows and was floored. When had we moved? I hadn't felt a thing.

Outside the ship, we were surrounded by a million stars. We had left the planet and were now cruising in an unknown direction. Our footsteps echoed across the metal walls and I continued to peer outside. Miles ahead of us, a blindingly bright ruby-red sun glowed, its yellow-orange flares beckoning us closer.

Finally, the end of the corridor opened into a large control room. Computer displays lined the walls, with several operators sitting at a few of the desks. A giant, glass windshield formed the far wall, reinforced with black beams stretching over the glass in a spider-web pattern.

In the furthermost left corner of the room, only a few paces away from the windshield, were two escape-pod hatches. We had a way out, at least... assuming we lived through whatever came next.

A waist-high control panel sat in the middle of the windshield. Another uniformed operator stood there, his hands resting on the controls. In the middle of the expansive room sat a large throne, like a highchair constructed out of woven-together burnt wires. My eyes spotted a pair of familiar wings.

Gordon, facing away from us, stood next to the throne. As we filed further inside, I glanced again at the main controls of the ship. Balil control systems appeared similar regardless of scale – the same basic configuration from our stolen shuttle appeared to be in place, here.

Lone clapping resounded in the room, bringing

my attention onto the throne. The highchair began to sway from side to side, its wires flexing like muscles.

"Thank you, for making things so much more exciting. Living as long as I have, it can be troublesome finding enjoyment," the voice of the Prince chirped.

The throne began to curl into a snake-like spiral, rotating and lowering down the Prince to our level, facing us. He was dressed in a new black-and-yellow-striped kimono, a blue rose tucked into the golden curls of his hair. As when we first encountered him, the only visible flesh was from his neck up.

The prince put his sleeve covered hands together and pressed them to his chin in a thinking gesture, "It's strange that you would come this far, to the point that you would even board my ship." He tilted his head and smiled, "Not that I'm discontent with you being here. It just comes across as very... suicidal."

He chuckled for a moment and pointed to his blue rose, "Speaking of suicide. Before you boarded, I ordered this to be brought to me. It's my own little bit of silly sentiment."

Bosun growled beside me, a low warning rumble coming from his chest.

The prince smiled at Bosun, "Such a beautiful shade." He stood up and walked to Gordon, reaching out his sleeved hand he prodded the dark blue wings.

His wasp yellow eyes were intent on the leathery folds of Pennon's wings, "I was informed that you had the lizard tied to a chair when my mercenaries attempted to recover him." Those bright, mad eyes flitted over to us.

"Your first impression was poor, yet now you people are grieving," he said and furrowed his brow.

"My name's Misique," his child-like face glanced at each of us in a shy manner.

Pierce calmly spoke, "Misique, we are here to get Gordon back to Manzala safe and sound."

Misique ignored the officer and turned towards me, "You wanted to preserve Pennon, did you not?"

I pressed my lips firmly together as to hold back my tongue, but I couldn't shift my eyes away from the Prince's.

The Son of Balil pouted, then looked at all the guards around him. A thought seemed to strike him, "Everyone out, my guests are afraid to speak openly with all these prying ears," he commanded.

Everyone but Misique, Gordon, and us three, shuffled down the corridor and into the elevator. Even the operators at the computers and the navigator at the main control panel stepped out. We were completely alone with the kimono-styled Prince and the altered Gordon.

Bringing his attention back to me, the prince smiled sadly. "Death is a terrible evil, but some would say that it's necessary," he sighed.

"Yer nonsense is making me sick, give Gordon back now!" Bosun snarled and spat.

Misique looked at Gordon with fondness in his eyes, "I'm giving him a gift, instead. We will become one. Don't you see how wonderful it is? Your precious brother will never have to die."

The canine's hackles stood on end and his lips pulled back exposing his bright white fangs, "Nobody can live like that, yah damned demon."

The yellow boy pouted and turned his gaze onto me once more, "Of course they can," he said, responding to Bosun but keeping his attention on me. "Just ask your friend, here."

Misique glumly shook his head, "You were able to forgive the rogue. Friends are a rare commodity to my people. We are vilified—simply because we have declared death as our enemy."

He stared down at my jacket pocket, in which my hand gripped the Black Box. My spine cringed, my whole body was electrified with fear. "And yet, so many have needlessly died because of you," I said, my voice shaking a little with each word.

The young boy shrugged and grimaced, "An unfortunate cost." Misique's eyes looked me up and down in a similar fond way he had stared at Gordon. "But, Death was coming for them anyways, at some point. And because of their sacrifice, I can drive Death away from others. You and I, we have the same enemy. And it should not be each other, I think."

My teeth were set on edge, whatever part of me his eyes passed over felt a shock of icy dread.

"Not everyone deserves eternal life, But you saw something in that hylathan that made you offer him a form of it," the prince said.

I looked away and towards the glowing stars in the front windshield.

"I would assume you've offered the same to others?" Misique asked in a gentle lulling tone. A delighted smile spread across the Prince's face, "You might as well be a Balil,"

My eyes snapped to the boy's penetrating stare in surprise.

He continued, "I could give you the real thing, you know. I could give whoever is dwelling in that device a form."

My imagination flared behind my eyes, an image of that brilliant cupid's bow smile and freckled skin. For only a moment in my mind, Jean was in my arms again in that summer sun.

Misique's grin beamed brightly, "We could be friends."

"We'd never," Bosun growled through clenched teeth.

Rolling his eyes the Prince said, "Well, I wasn't offering it to a mongrel like you. Martin? That's your name, correct? Calling you Aten would be too formal for friends, don't you think?" the Balil laughed.

The moment in my mind's eye with Jean had faded away and I was left feeling hollow. Intense need buzzed between my ears, the instinct to throw inhibition to the wind coursing through me. My memories flickered like an old neon sign, Jean, Glenmont, Jackson...Pennon.

"That isn't the point of all this," I whispered, reflexively, in a low tone.

Misique gave me a nonplussed looked, "What was that?"

"It's Martin," I said, bringing a smile to my face. "Misique, is that name French?" I amicably asked.

The boy laughed hysterically, Bosun stared at me, his jaw agape. Pierce gave me a sidelong glance.

Misique motioned me to come closer, "It's Latin...friend," the last word slid slowly from his lips in an elongated chilling exhale.

My stomach clenched anxiously as I moved forward, approaching the Prince. I stopped a few steps away and the boy closed the distance between us. It took everything in my power not to turn and run as we stood a mere six inches apart.

Looking up at me, the blonde boy slowly reached up and softly patted my left shoulder. The soft fabric of the kimono sleeve did not mask the solid, sharp quality of the hand inside. Even after his hand had dropped back down to his side, my left arm ached with a phantom pain caused by my distress.

"I knew you'd be interesting," Misique chuckled. "You'll see, you'll blossom beautifully with my aid."

"How soon will you be able to give me my Jean?" I asked.

The Prince's eyes crinkled happily around the edges, "We put Gordon together very quickly, your Jean will be a snap."

Bosun angrily took a step forward, only for Gordon to suddenly whip around in response to the threat to his handler. The altered man's eyes were filled with incredible sadness, the canine froze in place.

Pierce put his hands up and said, "Keep it calm."

The dog's hackles were raised, ears and jowls were pulled back angrily, but his tail was between his legs in fear. "What are yah doin' Martin? We're supposed to be saving Gordon," he snarled.

"Misique and I are saving him," I said, keeping my tone as level and pleasant as I could.

The furry one's eyes bulged in shock, his fists clenched in frustration. "We went through all this, just fer yah to turn?" Bosun's eyes teared up. He clenched his eyelids shut, trying to hold back his crying. "What the hell kinda monster are yah?" he huffed through the hot tears begging to roll down his face.

I went silent, I tried to maintain a blank look. Not reacting, not revealing how it hurt me to hurt him.

"Why didn't you stay below, Brother?" Gordon whimpered.

Bosun opened his eyes to gaze at his disfigured sibling, "I can still save yah. Yah can beat what's goin' on in yer head."

Tears slid down Gordon's grey face, "I don't want to see you like them, I don't want to see you in pieces."

The canine opened his mouth to respond, but Misique began to speak, "The first hurdle in our friendship is already here, Martin."

Gordon froze in response to the Balil's voice. Frozen fear weighed on my gullet, leaving me anchored in place. The Prince in front of me slithered over to his toy. Slowly reaching up, Misique's razor sharp metallic hand slipped out of his sleeve and extended to gently tussle the altered man's hair. Gordon didn't move an inch, only looking on with his panicked eyes at his brother. The disgustingly shiny black arm extended almost as long as the prince was tall, I wondered how he folded his arms under his kimono to hide them.

"My Gordon is nearly perfect," Misique turned a wretched scowl towards Bosun. "But as you saw at the test site, there are some kinks. Mainly, the mental blocks associated with his relationship with this beast." He patted his pet's head gingerly.

The muscular Xenoform took another anxious step forward, "Stop touching em' now!" he growled.

Rage flickered across the Prince's visage, "After seeing his reaction to this hound I realized that he is the final piece. Martin, I hope you understand what is necessary. Gordon's body is mine, but his mind is another story."

I took two steps backwards, looking back and eyeing the control panel. "It's unfortunate, but understandable," I said. I turned my head towards Misique, as he turned to look at me. An enthusiastic grin stretched across the young boy's cherub-like face, "Perfect," he purred. "Gordon, kill that measly dwarf and mutt."

The whirring sound from the altered man's body returned, the sound resonated around us and drilling into my ears. Gordon trembling and staring his brother down with mad eyes, tepidly stepped towards his two targets. The Dwarven Engine in his chest began to glow hot around the edges.

Bosun glared at his brother and widened his stance in preparation, "I won't fight yah, I'll hold onto yah fer however long it takes fer yah to fight this," he said. He put out his hands and readied to attempt a grapple.

"Please, get out," Gordon said, his voice wavering against the compulsion.

Pierce stepped closer to the Prince, his fists up. The Balil still facing me, tilted his head and rolled his eyes. Slowly turning to face the steely officer, Misique was no longer looking at me. I glanced again at the control panel.

"Get out!" Bosun's brother croaked.

Just as the Prince's pet lunged for his Xenoform brother and Pierce began to swing a fist, I sprinted for the control panel. As I passed the throne, I heard the sounds of clashing bodies behind me. I kept my focus on what was in front of me.

Loud grunts and the sound of fists thudding against flesh echoed in the room as I grasped the controls. Yanking on the steering rods, the ship jerked to the left. I struggled to hold on as our bodies attempted to follow Newton's first law of motion.

Glancing back, I saw Pierce latched onto the throne seat. The snake-like chair now stretched to the right side of the room. While the officer had successfully prevented himself from slamming into the right wall, the others were not so lucky.

The two grappling brothers lay atop three of the computers on the right, crushing the monitors and damaging the inner components to the point that they began to spit sparks. Misique lay against the door to the first escape pod.

The prince slid to the floor, the flower in his hair fell out, and he began to chortle manically. A screeching alarm began to pulsate throughout the hull. I watched the brothers wriggling, Bosun had managed to move onto Gordon's back. His burly arms were wrapped around the altered man's chest. The canine whined a little as his forearm pressed against the Dwarven Engine. His fur burnt and his flesh began to sizzle.

The prince picked himself off the floor, his yellow eyes looking at me from behind the hair that had fallen into his face.

"Was that your plan?" Misique taunted. "What was that supposed to do except make me angry, Martin?"

I frantically glanced at the control panel, looking for the button to open the escape pod doors. Pressing one button, a holographic map was displayed onto the windshield. I pressed another and the escape pod doors opened, the Prince gave me a confused scowl.

Jerking the steering rod again, the ship suddenly veered left and pushed us all to the right again. The small, kimono-wearing boy rolled backwards, and out of sight into the pod he went. I closed the door behind him.

Pierce let go of the throne and began running to the pod. If he'd made it in time—if he'd gotten to that launch lever before...but he didn't.

Loud bangs reverberated from behind the door. The dwarf reached out, but just as he was flipping the switch, the metal door tore slightly open by five razor sharp fingers. The escape pod launched, but Misique's black hand remained gripping onto the crumpled edge of the door.

The opening hissed as the inside of the ship was exposed to the vacuum of space. Once one of the ships outer panels sealed the opening, the only sound left was the blaring alarm.

The elevator down the corridor dinged and the loud shuffle sound of many feet hitting the floor barreled down the hallway towards us. I watched as the guards streamed in with their rifles.

"Don't move!" One of the uniformed mercenaries yelled.

Pierce and I put our hands up. Several guards moved to separate the wrestling brothers. They kicked at Bosun's exposed sides until he yelped and let go of Gordon. The altered man slowly stood up and stared at the Xenoform sprawled on the floor.

"Where's the Prince?" The same merc demanded.

The escape pod door made an ear-piercing scraping sound as the clawed hand bent the metal further open. I gulped anxiously. The guards instinctively pointed their firearms towards the noise.

My stomach dropped as a grotesque pin-point insect like leg stepped daintily out of the escape pod door. Barely audible clinking sounds were emitted, as several other skinny limbs made of blackened flesh webbed through cybernetic components crawled out. Another second past and he revealed himself.

A tall, lurking horror stood above us all. Barely draped in the yellow and black kimono, now tiny in comparison to the size of the creature's body, he grinned down at us. My mind tried to comprehend the collection of warped shapes in front of me.

A total of six monstrous and long limbs extended from the body. The four spider legs that supported him, and the two dangerously long arms that almost reached the floor. The torso reminded me of the throne, an interwoven mesh of blackened wires, bent about like a scoliotic spine.

With one of his inhuman arms he struck Pierce in the chest, slapping him with great force with the back of his hand. Wretched, snapping sounds filled the chamber over the steady rush of escaping air, followed closely behind the officer flying back and crumbling to the floor a few paces from the back wall. He weakly curled up and groaned in miserable pain.

Pierce tried to hold his head off the ground while he coughed up blood, his ragged breaths told me his broken ribs likely had punctured a lung. With one of his hands he patted his stomach, I remembered what he had hidden under his shirt. He hadn't dropped the grenade or magazine, but when the hell was he going to use them?

Even the Prince's mercenaries stared in fear as Misique's cherub face twisted into a horrific smile. The corners of his mouth reached up to the tops of his cheekbones; how his face was able maintain any semblance of human likeness before mystified me. Those wasp-like eyes focused on me, and I turned to frantically grasp the controls again.

It was only the blink of an eye that it took for him to reach me, it felt like something popped. I looked down, Jackson's end flickered in my mind and I realized I was now impaled. It was strange to me how the shock of it prevented any pain, at first.

Misique leaned close to my ear and whispered, "Don't worry, after this I'll take that little trinket of yours. I'll turn Jean and you into one of my little projects."

With a sudden swing I was thrown off his arm and across the room. My body slammed and rolled across the ground. Friction stopped my sliding right next to the lying Bosun.

The prince threw out his arms dramatically and

tilted his head back gleefully. "I'll stuff those AI's into your own bloated corpse! You'll get exactly what I promised you—be grateful, Martin," Misique said.

Gordon, standing over us, glanced at me. Dread washed over my brain as I looked upon our terrible fate.

TEN

"LET's get this over with. Gordon, end your dear brother," Misique said.

The Balil's pet coldly turned his empty gaze towards the canine. Bosun lifted himself back onto his feet and glared into the mad eyes of his disturbed brother.

"We're gonna get outta this together," the dog said.

The poor, altered man shook his head, "Don't let me see," he said.

Bosun put up his hands and flexed his immense muscles, ready to hold his brother back. "If my strength is good fer anything, I'll save yah!" he said, and lifted his thick shoulders in preparation to pounce.

Like a flash, the two launched for the other, their hands grabbing the other's arms in a test of power. Gordon's whirring got more intense, as the cybernetic muscles in his limbs twitched. Bosun gritted his fangs and snarled, his eyes looking deeply into the soul of his opponent.

The canine's feet slipped and began to slide

back across the floor, Gordon sheer force overwhelming him. My friend was going to have to get creative if he wanted to survive.

Bosun deftly released his grip and side-stepped; his brother lurched forward. Barely stopping himself from tipping over, Gordon used his forward momentum to whip around and throw a punch towards the canine.

From my position on the floor, and with my vision beginning to haze as I lost blood, it looked like a battle between titans. Huge giants, attempting to succeed over the other's will. Bosun leaned back, narrowly dodging his brother's fist.

Quicker than the strike of a praying mantis, the dog wrapped his hands around the swinging arm. The canine used his position to push all his strength into Gordon's punch, then directed it downward. The altered man tried to fix his stance in response, but it was too late.

Gordon tumbled to the floor, his cybernetics loudly clanging against the ground. His wings twitched wildly, uselessly trying to correct his current horizontal orientation. I was left in shock, every other time I'd seen Bosun fight he fought head on. It seemed like the old dog had, in fact, learned a new trick.

Misique yelled, "You can do better than that! Kill him!"

Gordon screamed, and his body convulsed in pain. Misique's words activated the electric shock that kept his pet in check.

The altered man finally stopped shaking and crying, he slowly got back onto his feet. "Can't see," he said hopelessly.

Bosun's ears pricked up and he smiled, "Yah won't, I promise," he said.

Gordon jumped towards the canine, swinging his fists wildly. Almost like dancing, the dog shuffled his feet and swung his upper body around. Skillfully avoiding every blow, he skipped his way to the front of the throne chair.

The altered man charged his brother; Bosun dropped low and lunged into Gordon's legs. Putting all his weight into knocking out his opponent's knees. Then lifting up, he utilized his brother's momentum again to launch him into the air and hurtling into the base of the throne.

Before Gordon could recover, Bosun sprinted to the seat of the throne and jumped in. Controlling the motion of the highchair with his weight, the canine shakily coiled the throne like a squeezing python around his brother. He'd been watching, I thought, resting my face against the cool floor. Bosun had learned.

The Balil's pet's arms were pinned to his sides and his wings crinkled as they were uncomfortably pressed to his back. His cybernetics whirred and revved to no affect; Bosun had him trapped.

My canine friend jumped down from the chair and turned to glare at Misique in defiance.

The prince, red-faced, stomped his spider-like appendages in insolent rage. "Grab the mutt now! Hold him down!" he demanded.

The surrounding mercenaries closed in on Bosun. I tried sitting up, but the hole in my stomach flared with pain and I feared whether my intestines would slip out. Pierce, struggling to breathe, pressed himself up in an attempt to get to his feet, but fell back down onto his knees.

Turning their rifles around to use the butts like clubs, they struck at the large canine. Bosun tried to dodge the many blows coming from all sides and grasped at their weapons. They encircled him, and thud after thud of metal against muscle brought Bosun to a desperate struggle, moving wildly trying to escape his entrapment.

He yelped as a rifle butt came down on his bandaged side, digging into his wound. His back curled and he dropped to one knee.

"Stop! Stop it!" I heard a voice cry out, only to realize it was my own.

A crack across the top of his head, dazed the poor dog and the many guards managed to get a hold of him. Keeping Bosun's arms behind his back and pressing his kneeling body down to anchor him. Eventually, the struggle simply...ceased.

Gordon, still trapped, wept incoherently at the sight of his brother being beaten. Bosun whimpered a bit, still conscious, but his eyelids drooped lazily as he struggled to focus.

"This is the kind of nonsense I have to deal with?" Misique said. His earlier tantrum morphed into the look of cold hatred across his face.

The prince calmly stepped over to the throne and sat in its chair, uncoiling it and freeing Gordon. The highchair went straight up and stood at its maximum height over us, with the monstrous Misique staring down at us.

Gordon got to his feet, his eyes never moving from his brother.

"Get on with it, you clumsy tin can," Misique

sighed, crossing his two front spider legs over one another.

The altered man stepped up to his brother, tears rolling off his grey sagging face. Bosun dazedly lifted his head up and looked at Gordon with his tired eyes.

"Don't let me see Bosun, don't let me see," Gordon cried. His nearly decaying flesh shaking around the icy metallic components that had been so brutally shoved into him.

"Sorry," the canine slurred.

Gordon's right hand clenched into a fist, "Don't let me..." his voice shook.

The fist slowly began to pull back, as the man choked on his tears.

Bosun shook his head and blinked hard, trying to stay awake. He looked straight up into his brother's eyes, "Love yah, Gordy,"

"Don't let me! Don't!" Gordon screamed, as the fist came down.

I watched with horror, wanting to look away but finding myself incapable of doing so. A thick crack, followed by crunching echoed in my ears.

The fist had made impact to the left side of Bosun's face, now it lay a few inches deep into my friend's shattered skull. Blood spurted out in a geyser, rushing past some of the exposed pieces of jagged bone. I helplessly gaped at this tragedy, wishing that it was me in my companion's stead.

He didn't deserve this.

The guards let the body drop to the floor and backed away. They seemed equally disgusted and afraid. Even they pointed their faces away from the scene, refusing to look at what cruelty they enabled to happen.

I glanced to Pierce, beginning to turn a shade of blue as he fought for each breath. I looked down at my own wound, the memory of Pennon's pyre lit up in my mind. Every terrible thing I had observed on this journey, could have been avoided.

This wasn't what we deserved.

I shifted my eyes to Misique, cruelly smiling as he watched our torment. Boiling rage filled my weakening body, with every fiber of my being I hoped the Prince would get what he deserves. I turned my attention back to Gordon, staring down at what remained of his brother.

It made my blood run cold, the twisted expression on his mutilated face. Eyes wide, filled to the brim with horror and insanity. Deep down, I think he knew there was no going back, no delusion would let him deny the head he just caved in.

Gordon's eyes flitted over to me, and I panicked.

Kicking my legs, I tried to push away from him, but the cold metal floor I was laying on was too slick with blood. I wondered how much of the fluids were my own, the searing wound in my gut flared with pain. Every part of my body felt cold and numb, except for the slash on my stomach that was throbbing with heat. Tears lined the rims of my eyes. He loomed over me, and his handler standing behind him broke into a broad smirk laughed and laughed.

The altered man's dead eyes looked through me, not registering my presence. He brought one of his hands to his face. His entire body was stock still, except for his trembling pupils.

Misique's laughing petered out and he said, "Well go on, take care of those two."

Gordon didn't respond, he simply extended index finger and thumb. With a quick jab, followed by a terrible wet pop, he began to gouge out his left eyeball.

The prince for the first time flinched and his face had a look of shock. "Stop! I was going to use those!" he whined.

The Prince's pet started to convulse, his muscles twitching violently in response to some kind of electric stimuli. His voice came out in starts and stops, "Didn't. Want to. See."

With his other hand he dug into his side, peeling back his metal implants to reach deeper. The sound was like digging a fork into a bowl of aluminum-foil-wrapped spaghetti, all tearing metal and sloppy noodles.

I cringed as he yanked out a device. It came out covered in a black sludge, and a few pieces of torn tissue still clung to the device's many sparking protuberances. He dropped the item and it thudded against the floor, rolling a few feet away. With that, he stopped convulsing.

Gordon was about to gouge out the other eye, when Misique jumped down from his throne and rushed to reach for his pet's hand. The altered man, slapped the prince's grasp away.

"Listen to me you heap of junk, you will stop this," the prince said, as he grabbed Gordon's wrist and slapped him across the face with his free hand.

The Balil's pet seemed unaffected by this blow, his empty left socket oozed vital fluids and his expression had turned angry. Eyebrows knitting together, as his remaining eye glanced at Bosun. The whirring started once more, but this time to such a volume it was almost like a plane's engine. The Dwarven Engine began to heat up again, turning a hot white so quickly that even Misique stepped back a little.

The prince scowled and his face turned a shade of red, "Don't you dare," he hissed.

"I didn't want to see," Gordon said, as he rotated his wrist to grasp the Prince's wrist. The two looked like they were practicing a forearm handshake.

Misique looked down at their arms and blinked in confusion.

With great force, Gordon clamped down on the Prince's wrist, and a crunching sound followed. The Balil tried to yank his arm away in a panicked manner, "You're really pushing it, Gordon," he said.

The prince looked up at the altered man's face and froze. The Balil's project cried, his salty tears mixing with the blood dripping down his face. His remaining eye glared at Misique with wide-eyed rage, his lips were peeled back in a snarl. He was hyper-ventilating and foam began to form at the corners of his mouth.

Misique swung his free claw at Gordon's head. The altered man responded by reflexively wrapping his free arm around the Prince's swinging appendage, pinning it to his side. The Balil dug his razor-sharp fingers into his pet's metal arms, the sound was like iron nails scratching against steel.

I gasped for breath, fighting the darkness that began to close around me.

With a mighty pull, Gordon closed the distance

between the two of them. Misique stumbled forward and the altered man took advantage by slamming his forehead into the button nose of his handler. I heard a muffled snap, and the boy's face bounced back from the force.

The Prince kicked his two front legs. The limbs struck Gordon's thighs, sinking into the exposed flesh, forcing the altered man to let go and take a step back.

Misique's broken nose gushed a black fluid, he tried to wipe it away with his crumpled wrist. He only managed to smear it across his rosy cheek; the liquid reached past his lips and dripped from his chin.

His wasp-yellow eyes crinkled joyfully at the corners, "I have to say. I'm very disappointed that I'll have to tear you to pieces, but—" he shrugged. "—I haven't had this much excitement in a long time."

The prince's body began to shake, "You all should be honored, you're about to witness the pinnacle of my people's necrotic technology!" he exclaimed.

The metal and flesh making up his body began to squirm like a thousand crawling maggots trying to find real estate in a festering wound. The Prince's sickly yellow aura flared around him. The light became so blinding, it was painful to look directly at him.

Gordon sprinted towards the prince, but a force hidden by the light blasted him back. The altered man's body slammed into several of the guards, the mercs yelped in surprise. The Dwarven Engine burnt into a screaming mercenary that was trapped underneath Gordon.

The others got up and stepped back beside their companions, gaping at their comrade's melting chest. The poor man tried to frantically push away, but the brilliantly white metal of the engine continued to sink into him.

Finally, it all stopped when his rib-cage crumbled and his organs boiled. Gordon lifted himself off the dead man, the only sound escaping the two the whirring and the sizzle of steaming flesh.

The mercenaries flinched back and glanced all around them; none of them seemed enthusiastic about going next.

My energy continued to slowly leak out of me, I was going to bleed out. I didn't care anymore. The more blood I lost, the more apathetic I became. I glanced at the control panel.

I put my hand in my pocket to check on the blackbox, I looked to the last escape pod. Pennon had been right, I let the past cast a shadow over me. I thought back to Jean's sunny smile, Bosun's wagging tail came up as well. My eyes welled up with tears, the woman we met on Altay appeared too. I glanced at Gordon, "Don't worry Bosun, I'll take care of him for you," I said to myself.

Trying to not draw attention to me, I slowly crawled towards the control panel. From here it felt like it was miles away.

Misique's yellow aura was dimming and his modified extremities were slowly revealed. The decaying flesh of his legs and torso had melded into a large serpents tail curled around him. His arms were shorter; however, he had used that surplus of length to form two extra arms.

It was like we were in the presence of Medusa herself, us feeble mortals turned to stone in our fright of the creature before us. Finally, his head. The previously taut, pink skin now sagged and stretched. His mouth a gaping maw, like a snake his jaw appeared unhinged. Those yellow eyes, no longer pleasant orbs resting in a pretty face, but disgusting stocks that extended out of the head, much like a snails eyes.

I felt a cold shiver run down my spine, I hadn't considered that he could become more insanely grotesque. I slightly quickened my final effort, dragging myself across the floor.

Gordon turned his one, mad eye towards the Prince, then sprinted towards him. Misique flicked his tail and lunged forward, with arms outstretched. With a deafening slap, the two collided. Trading blows, and grasping at any limb they could.

I had begun to pass the throne when I saw that the Balil was sneakily wrapping his tail around his pet, he was going to give a constrictor's squeeze when he was done. I pushed myself onto my knees to crawl faster.

Incoherent screeching and hissing came from the two brawlers, like the sounds of an alley cat fight taking place in a trash can. Suddenly, the trap was sprung and Gordon was being slowly crushed by the force of Misique's powerful tail. The altered man's yelling ceased, replaced with sputtering.

He strained against the rotten binding around him, his cybernetic components whirred louder and the engine burned brighter. The Dwarven Engine was being pushed to its very limits. It was already unstable as it is, only able to work through strange Balil jerry-rigging.

With his four arms, Misique wrapped them around Gordon's head in a caressing manner. "It's too bad, but I learn from my mistakes." He slowly brought his deformed maw to Gordon's ear, "Next time, I'll find a child instead. If I raise it myself none of those pesky emotions will get in the way," he chuckled.

Continuing forward, I was only a few moments away from reaching the controls.

"And what do you think you're doing?" Misique's voice called out.

My stomach twisted on itself and my wound throbbed with pain. I found myself at the base of the control panel and began the process of hoisting myself onto my trembling legs.

"Are you really so boring that you'll try that trick again, Martin?" The Prince asked in an annoyed tone.

I looked back; his focus was on me and I could see his tail loosen slightly. It must take concentration to keep it tight. He didn't even notice Gordon sliding his hands out from the Balil's iron grip.

"Useless. When I'm done here-" His voice cut short and was replaced with a violent tearing sound as Gordon's claws found their way to his torso and put all their strength into tearing him apart. He began to scream and writhe, but Gordon's immense, altered strength ripped him in half just above where his hips would have been.

The Prince's lower half curled and convulsed.

The severed tail rolled around as though trying to find its way back to the body. Gordon, taking advantage of the situation, threw himself onto Misique, and they both clattered to the floor.

I couldn't help but chuckle to myself, this is where not making friends gets you. I thought of Pennon and Bosun, in such a short time they had taught me so much. I also thought of Sylvester and felt a pang of guilt. He had tried to teach me the same and I treated him unkindly for it. How stupid was I to need all this to learn my lesson?

But it's wasn't too late, I glanced at the escape pod and became aware again of the experi-sense kit on my face. I swore to myself that I'd make things right, despite my ebbing consciousness.

The Prince struggled with his four arms to lift Gordon off of him, he punched and slashed at him with his razor sharp fingers. Cutting deep into both metal and graying flesh. The altered man extended his wings around himself to guard his body from some of the blows. The dark wings were growing ragged, like a tattered flag.

Gordon caught one hand and stomped his foot on the shoulder of Misique for leverage. He jerked on the arm with all his might. The limb snapped from its socket and the flesh ripped apart.

Gordon tossed the severed limb and the Prince flailed more erratically as his pet attempted to catch another arm. He trapped another swinging fist and like pulling the wings off a fly, the son of Balil lost another limb to his creation.

"Help me!" A horrified Misique yelled to the mercenaries.

Again, they glanced at each other, unsure as to

what the correct course of action was. They watched as another arm was stripped from their employer's body, and they seemed to come to a conclusion.

The guards began to shuffle their way towards the corridor, hoping to take the elevator to safety. Fleeting glances by the men looking over the Balil and his pet made it clear who they were betting on. So resolute in their prediction, they were willing to risk betraying Misique.

"Cowards! I'll see to it that you'll all be destroyed! You and your families!" Misique called after the mercenaries, as he was torn apart further.

Finally, the Prince stopped moving. Gordon halted his attack, kneeling over his former master looking at his blackened hands.

My heart leaped with joy, "Gordon, It's done," I said and smiled.

The altered man stood up and began to stride towards me. My smile dropped, as some nagging feeling tugged at the back of my brain. Was it his disfigurement that gave me the feeling of menace? Something in his demeanor had changed, a string snapped and then further frayed.

The whirring, it hadn't stopped. Dread pressed against my rib cage, aching to burst out. That sound he emitted was the only warning one got that he was ready to attack. Had he got stuck in that mode, unable to flip the switch that demanded bloodshed off?

He stared with his unblinking eye, and as he grew closer he pulled back a fist. I cowered back.

That's when one of the guards loudly

complained from down the hall, "Where the hell is the elevator?"

Gordon stopped in his tracks.

Another guard responded in a shaky tone, "You don't think the guys watching surveillance shut it down, do you?"

The altered man slowly turned to face the guards.

One merc noticed and began to yank on the elevator door trying to pry it open, "Shit. Shit. Shit!" he cried.

Gordon started his lumbering approach, his tattered wings and flesh hanging off of him like soaked tassels of mangled fabric.

"Bring up the goddamn elevator! I swear to god, please!" One of the men yelled into a radio. No one answered, "What the fuck! Answer me, do you want to be responsible for what's going to happen?"

I thought to myself, *"Responsible? What a time to be so concerned about responsibility."*

I immediately regretted my snarky inner commentary. The closer Gordon stepped, the more real their fate became. They were going to suffer horribly.

The ship filled with the sound of launching pods. The guards gaped out the corridor window, watching their fellow mercenaries abandon ship. The surveillance team had been watching, and just as the men in this room had decided, they, too, had mutinied. Word had moved fast, and the dwellers of this vessel were escaping in droves.

The many escape pods screaming past the hallway window and the front window I stood at fled in every direction, running away from their own decisions. I wondered why Misique hired them in the first place. He could have just as well had an army of undead slaves instead, if what he'd told me held true.

I thought back to his love of the dramatic, his need to quip and monologue. Zombies likely bored him to death, or maybe some part of him did want a friend? His definition of 'friend' was probably a disturbed one, but was it possible that even Balil Prince monstrosities get lonely too?

I must have lost a lot of blood, to find myself sympathizing with that creature. I shook my head. I need to get a hold of myself.

"The last pod, if we ran for it," a mercenary said, as Gordon stepped into the hallway.

The group began to squirm, taking frightened steps forward and back. Trying to figure how to sprint past the looming threat. It was no use.

The reinforced steel walls reverberated with heavy footsteps and screams, a real scene to behold. You ever hear the sound of rubber tires rolling through sloshed snow? That was the sound when he got his hands on someone.

I looked away and focused on my course of action. Glancing at the still struggling Pierce, I considered dragging him to the remaining escape pod.

The officer pushed himself up on his knees, as he gasped for air. He began to fumble with his shirt. My eyes were suddenly drawn to Misique, and my breath caught.

My mind had lapsed on an important detail about the sons of Balil, and I watched in horror as his body moved.

Pulling the broken pieces of his body to sit up, his lips curled like a Cheshire cat's. His disgusting wasp-like eyes flickered over us, as he laughed. A yellow orb began to protrude from his chest, he was preparing to escape us.

Like a small mirage the air in front of the Prince began to wave and morph, then it became like a mirror hanging in the air. It was a portal to his home-world.

Pierce shakily removed the grenade and magazine loaded with enchanted bullets. Holding the items in one hand, he crawled with his other three limbs to the prince.

Misique's smile dropped into an expression of pure horror. His stocky yellow eyes blinked at the loaded magazine, the bullets inside emitting a blue aura. Pierce was now right next to him, grinning from ear to ear.

"Good to know I'm actually going out like this," Pierce said breathlessly. Another coughing fit struck him, and he spit up more blood.

The Balil helplessly tried to wriggle away, trying to earn the moments needed to allow the orb containing his soul to get out of his body and into the portal.

Pierce clasped his hand on Misique's collar bone and pinned him down. "No witty remark, no threats? You've spent so much time running your gob and now you've shut it?" he said.

The doomed creature narrowed his eyes, and simply stared in pure hatred at my friend.

The steely-eyed dwarf glanced at me and solemnly nodded. With one movement, he activated the grenade, pressed both items to his chest and threw himself onto the pus colored orb.

I dropped to the floor and covered my head in expectation of the explosion. A few moments passed as I held myself there. Then--BOOM!

The blast rocked the whole room and my ears didn't even ring, the world simply went silent for me. I was certain I was now very deaf.

The explosion itself was fairly contained by Pierce's and Misique's bodies, it was the sonic spell on the bullets that did the majority of the damage. I looked up and saw the front window with its spider-web design cracked on all edges, making it appear even more like an arachnid's home.

The two of them had been blown to pieces and the portal was gone. I slowly stood up with much effort and noticed yellow shards sparkling like gemstones across the floor. An enormous weight lifted from my shoulders, Misique was dead.

But so was I.

Gordon was still tearing apart bodies in the hallway and was likely to come back to do the same to me. I glanced at the final escape pod, then to Gordon. He was going to roam this room for who knows how long, until either the Balils come here or allies arrive to keep the disturbed Balil creation caged for eternity.

I thought back to the tortured woman on Altay.

There was only one way to save Gordon. Looking out the window at the nearest star, I pulled the blackbox from my pocket. It was still working, still recording my consciousness. Still building a mirror image of myself out of ones and zeros.

I had no desire to call the copy of Jean I had created; even if I wanted to I had no ability to hear her. In my cowardice I had hoped to retain a semblance of what made her the woman I loved so dearly, to carry a map of her mind around like a trinket. A night light made of denial, to keep at bay my fear of the dark. My fear that she was really gone.

I only managed to let my fear live for me.

Cupping a hand over my numbing wound, I stumbled towards the escape pod. I pressed the button on the side to open the door. Then carefully with anxiously buzzing hands, I removed the experi-sense headset and blackbox. Gingerly placing the devices on the floor of the escape pod, I stood outside the door.

I felt ashamed I couldn't return Glenmont's Engine, that I couldn't return to personally tell Sylvester I'm sorry, and even more so for the deaths of my friends. But I had control of the ship...and nothing survives a trip into the nearest star.

The least I could do is tell my story.

...

Sylvester lumbered into the room, a heavy suitcase in each hand. Behind him followed a hylathan girl, her scales a beautiful, sapphire blue with teal speckles. She glanced around nervously, as she set her backpack down.

With a grunt Sylvester put down the luggage and tiredly waved to Dr. Glenmont, "Here you go, young lady. The Dr. Glen-," he looked at me and stopped in his tracks.

"He's back? Where-" Sylvester's voice trailed off, as he searched the room with his eyes.

Glenmont shook his head, "My apologies Sylvester, this is all that's left of him,"

Tears began to stream down his face, "No," he gulped. "You told me they found an escape pod," he said.

The inventor pointed at me, "and this was what was inside," he said. He nervously ran his hands through his hair, pushing the strands behind his ears.

I spoke, "Syl, I'm sorry."

Like a flipped switch, my friend clenched his fists and his expression turned to anger. "Don't you dare talk to me like you're him!" he spat.

"I've just finished explaining everything to Glenmon-" I was cut off by the hylathan girl.

"You're a copy of that Mr. Martin guy?" she asked.

Glenmont stepped forward, "He is, I'm sorry that our meeting has to be so stressed. It may be for the best if you wait in your room, Pinion."

Pinion nodded, "I just wanted to ask. If my dad...did he die for something?"

"He sacrificed himself for a friend," I answered.

The girl smiled sadly, and let out a quiet laugh. Tears lined her bright amber eyes, her father's eyes. "Sounds like him," she said.

"I- I'm sorry," Glenmont began to stammer.

Pinion put up her index finger to her lips, in a silencing gesture. The inventor fell quiet, as he looked at his newly adopted daughter.

"It'll be alright. Thank you, Mr. Martin." She nodded at her adoptive father. "I'll take my stuff to my room, sir," she said.

The young girl picked up a suitcase and began to lug it out of the room.

"You can ask the droids if you need anything," Glenmont said, placing his hand to his forehead.

"Got it," Pinion called from the hallway.

The dwarf anxiously sighed and turned back to me, "I know it doesn't mean much, considering I'm talking to a box right now." He began to rub his tired eyes, his face looked a little puffy too. "But I don't hold it against you for failing to return my engine, I should never have risked your life for an object," his voice cracked a little.

Being essentially a program didn't mean I couldn't simulate emotions, I felt empathy for this man. He looked sick with guilt, I wished I could do more, but that wasn't my place. It would only be cruel to cast a shadow over his life, which was why I was going to ask Slyvester something important.

"Syl?" I asked.

He didn't answer.

"I know I'm not owed any favors; I am only Martin in concept. I'm an impression in this blackbox and not really your friend," I paused to see whether he'd answer, he didn't.

"But, you were right when you told me-," I stopped for moment. "When you told Martin when he was alive, that he needed to let go. He did, but I'm still here and so is Jean's AI," I said.

My friend relaxed his hands and his anger turned back to sadness. Lip quivering, he asked, "And what about you?"

If I had a heart, it would be breaking in this moment. "Martin had a final wish. He wanted to prevent me lingering in people's lives, like how he had allowed the copy of Jean in his," I said.

Sylvester threw out his hands in frustration, "So you want me to erase you? To delete the evidence that my friend even existed?" He tried to wipe away the tears and hold back his sniffles. "Your plan from the start was to have this, right? You and Jean are together in there and you want me to delete you?" he said.

"The both of us," I said.

"Why?" he sobbed.

"Because," I said, "we don't have a place here. We aren't the point of all this."

He blinked in confusion, "The point of what?"

"Living."

ABOUT THE AUTHORS

BETHANY (BENNY) LOY is a burgeoning author residing in Washington State. She has published two short stories and this novella, a promising start for just beginning her professional writing career in late 2018. In her free time she plays video games, snuggles her cat Hawk, and daydreams about owning a dog she'll name Toucan. She hopes to produce thought-provoking pieces in the future.

FROG JONES began co-writing with his wife Esther in 2011, and the two have been rising stars in the science fiction/fantasy literary world ever since. He is currently the acquisitions editor of Impulsive Walrus Books. He has been running tabletop RPGs since he was 11 years old, has an extensive board game collection, and is an old-school veteran of the anime sub/dub wars. He's written many things; most can be found at www.jonestales.com.

CPSIA information can be obtained
at www.ICGtesting.com
Printed in the USA
FSHW021220250220
67414FS

9 781732 247727